A Soldier's Reunion
Cheryl Wyatt

Steeple
Hill®

Published by Steeple Hill Books™

STEEPLE HILL BOOKS

Steeple
Hill®

Recycling programs
for this product may
not exist in your area.

ISBN-13: 978-0-373-87532-0

A SOLDIER'S REUNION

www.SteepleHill.com

Printed in U.S.A.

Not possible. Can't be him. Can it?

Warmth radiated from a presence behind her. She inhaled deeply and forced the shock from her face. She used every ounce of strength to slowly turn around.

The instant his eyes lit on her face, his mouth slid open.

He stared.

Mandy stared.

Though his impressive frame was that of a man instead of a boy now, she'd know him anywhere.

"Nolan?" She hated the breathlessness in her voice. Despised the tears stinging at the sight of him. The welcome sight.

No.

Only because he's rescuing you. Not because he's Nolan, the only man you've ever loved.

Eyes as kind as she remembered explored her face. He seemed unable to speak for a moment. Or blink.

"Manda Panda?" It came out as a whisper.

The spoken name shot pain through her heart.

She didn't want to hear it. No one had the right to call her that anymore. Especially not him.

Books by Cheryl Wyatt

Love Inspired

*A Soldier's Promise
*A Soldier's Family
*Ready-Made Family
*A Soldier's Reunion

*Wings of Refuge

CHERYL WYATT

An RN turned stay-at-home mom and wife, Cheryl delights in the stolen moments God gives her to write faith-driven action and romance. She stays active in her church and in her laundry room. She's convinced that having been born on a naval base on Valentine's Day destined her to write military romance. A native of San Diego, California, Cheryl currently resides in beautiful, rustic Southern Illinois, but has also enjoyed living in New Mexico and Oklahoma. Cheryl loves hearing from readers. You are invited to contact her at Cheryl@CherylWyatt.com or P.O. Box 2955 Carbondale, IL 62902-2955. Visit her on the Web at www.CherylWyatt.com and sign up for her newsletter if you'd like updates on new releases, events and other fun stuff. Hang out with her in the blogosphere at www.Scrollsquirrel.blogspot.com or on the message boards at www.SteepleHill.com.

In his heart a man plans his course,
but the Lord determines his steps.
—*Proverbs* 16:9

To my critique partners and prayer sisters: Pamela James, Cynthia Hawkins, Michelle Rogers, Danica Favorite-McDonald, Camy Tang, Robin Miller. I am thankful for your honest assessments and encouragement. Can't wait until we all share shelf-space.

To my parents, Bill and Lois Blankenship. I struggle to craft characters with traumatic pasts and dysfunctional families because I was so fortunate to have been born to the two of you. You have encouraged every step of my journey and championed my dreams. I love you and know you love me.

To Melissa, Krista, Sarah, Joan and the Harlequin team for making my books shelf-worthy. You are incredibly talented.

To God, thank You for reuniting us when we stray. That you are a God who chases is amazing. Thank You for getting me through the bumps in this story's road.

To Billy, my personal hero, for filling our home with hilarity and for being so laid-back you're horizontal when the house goes askew under deadlines.

Chapter One

"Briggs, phone! Chief Petrowski's on the line. Says it's beyond urgent."

U.S. Air Force Pararescue Jumper Nolan Briggs rushed past teammates Brock Drake and Vince Reardon, who stopped rigging parachutes and looked up. The airmen grew sniper-still and spotter-alert as did the other PJs in Refuge, Illinois's skydiving Drop Zone facility.

Nolan grabbed the DZ phone from teammate Chance Garrison. "Briggs speaking."

"Nolan, I'm tasking your team to a major bridge collapse."

Nolan pressed the phone tighter against his ear and processed Petrowski's words wafting across the line. "Major bridge collapse? Where?" Adrenaline pumping, Nolan eyed his teammates.

They stood at his words and marched close in listen-mode.

"Reunion Bridge over Refuge River—hold on," Petrowski said.

"Refuge." Nolan hiked his chin to his team while on hold.

The room erupted in activity as airmen grabbed gear.

Nolan had been placed in temporary command while PJ team leader Joel Montgomery traveled abroad with his wife to meet children they were adopting. Second-in-command, Manny Péna, was in surgery to remove pins, following a two-year-old injury incurred during a skydiving accident.

Nolan yanked a notebook from PJ Ben Dillinger's pocket. As Petrowski, back on the line, talked about the rescue mission, Nolan scribbled information.

Stiffening beside Nolan, Ben straightened. "Hey, babe," he called for his fiancée, Amelia, near the round tables across the room. She approached, Ben's brother Hutton following, his Mosaic Down Syndrome causing his eager feet to shuffle.

"Didn't Reece have a field trip today, across the bridge at the museum?" Ben said of his stepdaughter-to-be as he grabbed Amelia's hand.

"Yes." She scanned the note. Her face turned pasty. "Th-they would have been on the way back. P-probably on the bridge."

Arms numbing, Nolan tightened his grip on the phone as he observed Ben and Amelia. Dread pounded through his body, incinerating the lining of his gut.

The room stilled as implications of Amelia's words sank in. Ben's arms steadied her. "Don't panic. We don't know for sure she was on the bridge when it went."

"What if she was?" Amelia, trembling, slid to a chair.

Nolan squeezed Amelia's shoulder with his free hand. "We'll handle it. Okay? I guarantee Refuge divers are already there."

Amelia managed a catatonic nod. Ben searched Nolan's face. The only other time Nolan had seen Ben look this rattled was when his father passed away last year.

Nolan leaned close to Ben. "Stay with her 'til you hear from me."

Blinking rapidly, Ben looked torn. "We're already two men short. If I don't go, that puts you at only four."

"We'll make do. I can use you here for now. Run the command post. Once we see Reece is okay, you can join us on the bridge."

Ben gave a short nod. "I'll call the church. Tell folks to pray. Refuge hasn't experienced anything like this in its history that I'm aware of. And we don't know who all was on that bridge…" Ben's composure faltered.

Nolan knew Ben loved little Reece as though she were his.

"Don't buckle, Dillinger. Keep your head. Make sure our airmen's families are accounted for. Have everyone wait here at the DZ or Refuge B and B. Cell and landlines will be jammed from mass calls going in and out."

Nodding, Ben slipped a bronze arm around his wife-to-be.

Shoulders hunched, Hutton chewed his tongue and blinked close-set eyes while shuffling near. "I praying too, Benny."

"Thanks, buddy." Ben hugged his brother, then faced Nolan. "Can we load? I'll help with that at least."

Nolan covered the phone and nodded.

Two minutes later, gear in arms and courage in their steps, the PJs were out the door.

The harrowing look in Ben's eyes echoed the sentiment screaming through Nolan's mind: had Reece been on that bridge when it collapsed?

"How bad is it?" Nolan asked Petrowski as they sprinted to the waiting chopper minutes later.

"Pretty bad." Aaron Petrowski, commanding officer of their team plus two others, answered above rotor noise. "Bridge collapsed in a V." Aaron heaved an extraction basket hoist into the craft. "Expecting mass casualties if we can't get those people off."

Nolan paced his breathing as he tossed heavy medical packs into the belly of the bird. Diving gear and rescue equipment loaded, Nolan climbed in, followed by his other three teammates.

Petrowski hunkered in and faced the opening. "Where's Ben?"

"Tell you in a minute. What else?" Nolan signaled the pilot to take them up.

Petrowski studied him. "There's a flammable tanker about to boil from flaming cars. If heat expands it, she'll blow."

"Cars near enough to ignite it should something spark?" Nolan asked above howling wind as the chopper lifted.

"Yes. Unfortunately, so is an elementary school bus."

Vince swore softly.

Pulse kicking, Nolan's gut clenched. "Full of little kids?"

Petrowski nodded. "On their way back from a field trip."

Nolan's stomach hollowed. "The reason I had Ben stay behind for now is because his stepdaughter-to-be might be on that bus."

Petrowski's head jerked around. "You serious? Little Reece?"

Anxiety for Ben and Amelia fought for rabid hold but Nolan steadied himself. "Yeah."

As if their team hadn't already been under enough pressure with the possibility of Nolan being plucked from it. No one voiced it, but everyone felt it. Any mission, starting with this one, could be Nolan's last with the team, thanks to superiors wanting to use him elsewhere.

Sighing, Petrowski slid a hand over his silvery-blond buzz. "News air surveillance report a dozen children are on it."

"Can we have the news chopper megaphone them off the bus?"

Petrowski stretched out his legs. "Problem with that is there's no place safe for them to go should the tanker blow. Unless all the cars burn themselves out, that's a mammoth possibility."

Brock's head tilted toward Nolan and Petrowski. "Plan?"

Paper spread over the floor, Nolan diagrammed. "Lift kids in rescue baskets here. Two pararescuemen per litter. Work fast."

"So, what exactly happened? Any word on that?" Brock shifted closer to hear over the chopper blades whipping air. The Pave Low's engine noises gurgled up the southern Illinois sky.

"A small aircraft flew into the support beams near where the bridge connects to land," Nolan answered.

"Steel beams are bending under the pressure. Concrete's crumbling. Engineers at the scene say the bridge is tilting an inch every five minutes. Any second, the rest could give way. At this time nothing short of prayers will brace up that bridge."

He eyed the team. "Refuge divers got to most cars that slipped into the water and helped people out that could be."

"And those that couldn't?" Nolan asked.

"Couldn't be helped." A grim cloud camouflaged Petrowski's face.

"I hope someone has the sensibility to get the kids off the bus. Though the tanker's volatile, they probably have a better chance off than on. Even minor shifts could hasten its plunge," Nolan said.

Petrowski brushed a hand over his forehead. "Worse thing they could do is get off then back on the bus for any reason." He eyed Nolan. "Pray the bridge holds until we get there. Can't land a chopper on it, so we'll rappel rigs in teams of two."

Nolan ignored Vince's smirk at Petrowski's praying comment. Team brotherhood was stronger than personal feelings.

Once they hit the bridge, everyone would be about the mission.

Screams of a dozen children drifted through the smoke and clamored for Mandy Manchester's attention.

Disregarding her own pain and fear, she scrambled through mazes of twisted metal, forcing her feet across puddles of burning gasoline. "M-must get to them. Please help me."

But who was listening? No one. Not for a long time.

Today, today please hear me—for them.

Determination compelled her beyond an overturned truck. Its driver lifted himself from the cab. He'd be okay, she decided as she ran past. The dawning sight of a crumpled orange school bus clenched her stomach.

Using her uninjured hand, she pried open the door. Fought to cover her mouth at the sight of the driver's forehead, lacerated like the interstate. She was a doctor-in-training! Think she'd have learned to control outward reactions by now. She rushed to press his shirt hem to the angry knot.

"Be okay. Just a little bump," he slurred.

Little? Hardly. "Hold pressure here. Don't let up, okay?" She spoke in calm tones but a take-charge voice. He'd need at least five stitches. So would she, but who was counting?

"I'm a doctor. Who's hurt the most?" Mandy moved on to two adults who identified themselves as teachers. One rested a hand on the other, slumped over.

"Her neck hurts." She peered at Mandy with wide eyes.

"Hold her neck like this and keep it still. Carefully walk her to an area where you'll be seen by First Responders." Mandy demonstrated by placing the teacher's hand on her cohort's neck and jaw. She helped them outside before returning to the mounting pandemonium on the bus, which leaned so far left it felt like it would soon topple over the gaping bridge.

Something inside her screamed to get these children out. Triage training kicking in, she maneuvered down the aisle. Even with careful movement, the bus shifted several inches. Screams cut the air in tones resembling ambulance sirens.

Halted and heart pounding, Mandy grasped a green spongy seat with her good hand. She faced the tousled group.

Several frightened eyes stared back.

"Is anyone hurt bad enough they can't walk?" At her voice, hysteria hushed to whimpers.

A dozen little heads looked at themselves, then all around. Disheveled hair shook and tiny trembling mouths warbled, "No."

"This is terrible and scary, I know. But we're going to get you to safety, okay?" One by one, Mandy took the hands of the littlest ones and matched them with those of an older child.

"Let's make a game of it. Like a reverse Noah's ark. Two-by-two." She ushered each duo out the doors. Once all visible children were off the bus, Mandy directed them to the safest-looking intact portion of the bridge.

Surely authorities knew by now it had collapsed. Surely they knew, and help would be here soon. Though it seemed an hour had passed already, probably only minutes had.

After triple checking over every seat of the bus for unconscious children, Mandy helped the driver off. She assisted him to lie down flat near the teachers and joined the huddle of traumatized children.

"H-how will we get off the bridge?" One little girl eyed their surroundings. Burning cars looked to be melting into the kind of tanker that transported flammable gas. It blocked one exit. A gaping hole the size of Refuge Memorial's pediatric ward blocked the other.

She faced the trembling child. "What's your name, sweetheart?"

"J-Jayna."

"I'm Mandy. I'm training to be a doctor. What do you want to be when you grow up?"

"A-a teacher."

"Good choice. I want you to think about how you would decorate your very first classroom, okay? Think about it *really* hard. Then I want you to tell me all about it once we get off this bridge. Okay? I'll want every little detail."

Jayna nodded vigorously, eyes still big with fear.

One boy stepped forth. "I wanna be a fireman. They help people." He took the little girl's hand. "Especially people who are very frightened."

Mandy smiled. "What's your name?"

"Caden," the boy said.

"Caden, you'll make a grand fire chief some day."

Please let them live to fulfill their destinies.

"Are there people in the cars?" Jayna's voice escalated.

"No. Thankfully, it looks like everyone escaped before the cars caught fire." Mandy pointed up the bridge. "See? All those people huddling together? They can't get to us, but they'll keep each other calm. That's what I need you to do, too, okay?"

Caden leaned nose to nose with Jayna. "Yeah. We gotta get as brave as the big people. Can ya?"

She nodded and swiped a finger across her nose.

Another girl in a glittery "Princess" logoed shirt moved close and handed Jayna a tattered brown bear. "Here. Bearby will make you brave."

Mandy's heart melted at the little child with teddy-bear-big eyes who looked like she longed to snatch the well-used toy back for herself. "That was nice, sweetie. What's your name?" Mandy asked the girl who clasped Jayna's other hand.

"Reece North. And I want to be a famous rock star with big pink glasses and diva rhinestones when I grow up."

Smiling, Mandy faced the others. "Caden is right. Think you can be that brave?" A bouquet of miniature heads nodded.

Except one. "I got asthma. Smoke makes it hard to breathe." He audibly wheezed. But his color seemed okay. For now.

Mandy pulled him close. "Do you have your inhaler?"

His arms clasped her neck. "On the bus. I think."

"My face feels sunburned," another child said. Mandy noticed. All their cheeks resembled rubies from fire heat. She eyed the bus. Maybe it would be better, safer to get them back on. That way, she'd have the inhaler should the little guy's asthma kick in. Plus, they'd be more shielded from smoke. Then if the tanker exploded, they might be protected from the blast and debris.

Or, putting them back on the bus could help them to die in one unit. Dread sickened her at the thought that any decision she made might hasten the manner of their deaths.

Drowning or burning. Which was worse?

Please show me what to do. I don't know what to do. I just know I don't want them to die.

"H-how will we get off the bridge?" Jayna persisted.

"Experts will know whom to send and what to do." She'd been in Refuge long enough to know its townsfolk would pull together and rise above this epic tragedy.

"I want my mommy!"

"How will Daddy find me?"

"Who will come for us?" Jayna persisted.

Mandy tugged as many of them close as would fit, even though it hurt like mad to move her hand. The others huddled in, looking at her like she was their one and only lifeline.

They're looking to me. But it has to be You. Send help. Hold up this bridge, and hold down the fires.

Peace she hadn't felt in a decade befell her. Thankful He'd heard, and confident He'd act, she met each child's frightened gaze. Then smiled into each face, using her eyes and—okay, mental prayers—to infuse courage, instill hope and inject calm.

"Someone strong and brave will come. I promise. Someone who rescues people all the time."

"Who?" Jayna's voice persisted. "Who will come rescue us?"

Mandy looked square into two frightened, tearful eyes and said with calm assurance, "Only the best."

"There it is." Nolan observed the unimaginable chaos. His pulse ramped at the surreal devastation.

"Whoa!" Chance's mouth hung open. The team stood as one unit, observing the collapse from the air.

Vince inclined his torso. "Unbelievable."

"Weird to see steel and a slab of concrete we've driven over time and time again..." Brock shook his head. "Just—gone."

"Okay, guys. Gear up." Nolan grabbed his stuff and lined up at the door. If he was gonna lead his team, he was gonna lead them. Joel was the kind of commander who hit the trenches alongside his men. Nolan would follow Joel's stellar example of being both a humble servant and a confident leader.

As if reading his mind, Petrowski leaned over. "Being Tech Sergeant in charge, you don't have to go, Briggs."

"With all due respect sir, if my brothers are gonna be in harm's way, I'm gonna be in it as well." Wasn't that what their creed was about? "So others may live?" Even at the risk of losing their own lives for people who may never know it?

Petrowski nodded. "Then if I can remember how to perform rescues with a hoist basket without plunging to my death, I'll be there too."

Vince laughed. "You've been sitting behind a desk rescuing your solitaire games too long is my bet."

Petrowski's laugh infiltrated the air. A sound seldom heard the past couple years. "Not solitaire. FreeCell. It'd do me good to get back in the real game. With you guys."

Heavy silence ensued as the men tossed glances of respect toward Petrowski. He'd lost his wife tragically two years ago and hadn't been on the field since. He'd taken time off to regroup and be there for his boys. No one blamed the new widower and suddenly single parent of twin babies for backing out of the dangers that came with pararescue.

Now, Petrowski was trying to do everything in his power to keep Nolan on the team. And that meant coming back.

"We can manage without you. Your call, though," Nolan said.

"Real question is, could you manage *with* me faster?"

Nolan tossed him rope and a set of gloves. "Absolutely."

Petrowski donned the gear. "Let me brief the pilots and Central Command, and I'll be down there."

They secured headsets, by which they'd communicate. Test clicks sounded. His team would work together like a well-oiled machine gun. Rapid. Precise. Ready for any complication. And, as with any mission, there'd be at least one.

"Showtime. Let's go." Nolan stepped over the edge. Pave Low hovering above, the team, stringed like black beads on a silver strand, hoisted to the barely-there bridge. Once flat-booted on it, they circled their temporary leader for instructions, then commenced duty.

A barge with firemen and trucks extinguished blazes and sprayed cooling chemicals on the tanker. Nolan quickly cleared his area. Near the checkpoint, he found Vince and Petrowski.

"River Guard divers have it under control there." Vince scanned the water. "I'm hanging back to be sure though."

"Aaron and I are heading to the other side to make sure they got all the kids to safety. Meet us at the DZ debrief later."

Vince gave a thumbs-up symbol. Nolan signaled the pilots to drop hoist ropes. He locked his legs around it and held on as it went airborne, dangling Nolan and Aaron across the chasm of destruction. Closer, Nolan peered through high-powered military binoculars at the remnant of people.

His eyes lit on one, surrounded by a handful of children. He blinked. Nearly slipped. He tightened his grip on the binoculars. Shock jolted through him.

Mandy? Memories assaulted him.

The woman looked exactly like his high school sweetheart. The one his dreams had never let him release. The one no other woman competed with in his heart. *Looks like her but it can't be*, his mind mumbled, fumbled with the possibilities of this happening. She looked familiar enough to elicit an old ache. Yet different enough for doubt to detonate the crazy notion.

His Mandy smiled more. This woman's frown seemed set in stone and engraved on her face.

Except when she tended to a huddle of children. The granite softened. Granted, she'd just been in probably the most harrowing ordeal of her life. But the underlying sadness cloaking her face was different. The longevity of lines pulling her mouth into a frown had been there awhile. A long while. Like she hadn't smiled in forever.

The helicopter hovered near the split. The pilot lowered Nolan directly above where tons of concrete entombed cars…and people so he could call an "all clear" of the area. His soles brushed the broken bridge. The broken bridge brushed his soul. He let go of the hoist and unclamped the safety latch. Pausing to wait for Aaron, Nolan scanned the shredded waterway for the woman he'd seen from the air.

The woman who looked like Mandy. Good, they'd gotten her, the teachers and remaining children off the bridge. After calling "all clear" into his headset, he signaled the pilot to take him to the drop point, a nearby parking lot.

Once down, he jogged over. Awesome. All the children looked uninjured. She talked while assessing them. Her voice was as he remembered. Deeper maybe. Dark hair escaped a frazzled twist at her neck. Her hand patted it, her efforts only loosening hair from the stylish utensil holding it. Nolan smiled. Until he saw her other hand. The left angle indicated fracture. Yet she worried with her hair. Typical Mandy. If this was indeed her. Only one way to find out.

He nodded to the child she faced and approached her from the back. Petrowski strode past to where Chance knelt, securing a respiratory mask to a wheezing child while Brock held him.

"How's it going over here?" Nolan asked.

The woman jerked at his voice. Had to be her. Only one way to be sure.

Nolan spoke their secret code.

Chapter Two

"Manda Panda," a voice said softly behind her.

Mandy's spine stiffened. Children giggled. She froze. Military-buzzed heads lifted to stare.

Again, the voice from moments before, and years before, suctioned the last pocket of air from her lungs.

No one had called her that in ten years. Ten.

Not possible. Can't be him. Can it?

Warmth radiated from a presence behind her. Slightly ragged breathing. Maybe hers and not his. Hard to tell. She felt like she orbited in a pre-surgical anesthesia vortex all of a sudden. She inhaled deep, cleansing breaths and forced the shock from her face and neck. She used every ounce of strength to slowly turn around.

The instant his eyes lit on her face, his mouth slid open.

He stared.

Mandy stared.

Though he was more filled out and his impressive frame was that of a man instead of a boy now, she'd know him anywhere.

"Nolan?" He had to notice her voice sounded like a ventilator gone bad. She hated the breathlessness. Despised the tears stinging at the sight of him. The welcome sight.

No.

Only because he's a rescuer. Not because he's Nolan, the only man you've ever loved.

Eyes as kind as she remembered explored first her face, then her body, but not in a sensual way. He seemed unable to speak for a moment. Or blink.

"Manda Panda?" It awed out as a whisper.

The spoken name streaked emotional pain through her.

She didn't want to hear it. No one had the right to call her that anymore. Especially not him.

She lifted her chin. "Mandy." She hadn't meant it to be so curt.

Hurt fluttered in his eyes. Then confusion. Disappointment. Concern. Maybe even a little irritation.

He stepped toward her. Ran a hand over his dark-blondish buzz and left it there as he took another slow step. He blew out a forever breath. "I can't believe it's you."

He didn't blink or take his eyes off her. His gaze reached her hand. "You're hurt." He took another step toward her.

Her muscles stiffened. *Cold. Be cold. This is the man who broke your heart and never looked back. Never called, never—*

She stood rigidly and lifted her shoulders. The way she did when she wanted to look in control, in charge, and professional at the hospital. When she called a cardiac arrest code and needed family and nurses carrying her out her life-saving orders to believe she knew exactly what she was doing. Though she might be scared crazy. No one else needed to sense the emotion inside. Things went better for everyone that way.

He glanced around. "All children were removed okay?"

She blinked. "Children?"

He motioned a vague hand toward the bridge.

Heat rushed her face. "Oh. Yes. Yes." She nodded at his uniform…that he more than sufficiently filled out. "Men, dressed like you, lifted them in baskets to helicopters." She tried not to stare like a dolt. He really could be a poster boy for a military exercise regimen. Gone were those lanky arms and chicken legs she used to tease him about.

She tried to ignore how strong and eerily familiar he felt as he guided her to sit on a padded cooler full of ice and water bottles. His team had lowered it from a helicopter after rescuing everyone from the bridge.

His gaze danced down her face and lit on her neck. His jaw slackened. Lines around his eyes creased as he leaned in.

The panda necklace! That he'd given her at age sixteen. *So you'll never forget me,* he'd said.

Her hand snaked up to clench it. Too late. He'd seen.

Surprise glittered over his face. "You still have it." It came out more like a statement of disbelief than a query.

Not wanting to look like an idiot, Mandy slipped her hand from it. "It softens the children toward me in the hospital, makes them less afraid."

As if sensing her discomfort—and her omission of the main reason she couldn't take it off—he politely averted his gaze.

She tried not to look at his left ring finger, though it called to her like an emergency page on night shift. Forced herself not to care that his finger had no ring. Or how soft, warm and capable his hand felt as it brushed expertly over her injuries. He obviously knew what he was doing medically, not just what he was doing to her emotionally.

"Hurt anywhere?"

How ironic the question. Bottomless eyes bored into hers. "Mostly my wrist." *Mostly.*

He ceased staring only to check those areas. Leaning closer, he lowered his voice. "Look, Mandy, I know this is awkward. If you'd rather someone else—"

"I'm fine." For the most part. What else could she say? Admit her heart still ached from ten-year-old trauma? No. She refused to show herself weak around him again. He'd seen her at her most vulnerable, then rejected and abandoned her. She could never put herself in that position again.

Not liking his knowing, penetrating visual inquiry, she glanced at his uniform. "I see you made it through boot camp."

That caused him to laugh.

"Barely." He splinted her wrist then wrapped a sling around her arm. "You know how I was never a morning person. Those o'dark-thirty wake-up calls nearly did me in."

She fought nostalgia with a vengeance.

"I see you made it through med school." Pride sparkled as his eyes viewed the title embroidered on her rumpled scrubs.

She nodded because the emotion in his words disabled her voice.

"I'm proud of you, Mandy." His smile gleamed genuine and warm. His gaze lingered, reaching deep, almost desperate, as if searching for something lost. Yet glowed radiant as in fascinated wonder of something found.

Heat came to her cheeks. She averted her gaze. How had she forgotten how deep his dimples were? How smooth and suave his voice. And how exquisite his eyes.

Cold. Be cold.

Do. Not. Thaw.

She lifted her chin. She supposed he made it through pararescue training, otherwise he wouldn't be here. Must have been one of those brave, uniformed men making a grand entrance from helicopters. Both of which had enraptured the children's attention, and helped them momentarily forgo their fears. Had even caused her to forget for a few moments they were all on the brink of death.

How would an elite, world-class airman end up in a small town calamity? Did he live nearby?

Oh, please no. She forced herself to stop wondering about him, the one thing on earth that could undo her and unravel her future. She'd ask Miss Ivy, town matriarch, landlady and owner of Ivy Manor where Mandy lived. She straightened her shoulders and spine and adopted a professional air.

He studied her carefully, almost comically. As if he knew her drill. Using coping mechanisms to prove to both of them his presence wasn't affecting her.

"I see you're still military." She eyed emblems on a maroon beret, peeking out his side pants pocket.

"I see you're still Manchester." His gaze dealt heavy inquiry as it dipped to brush her name tag before reaching for her face again. The tender way his eyes held hers reminded her of an all-consuming embrace. *His* embrace.

She swallowed. Of course she'd never married. Why would she after having her heart ripped out and stomped on by his proverbial combat jump boots? What business was it of his?

She shoved to her feet before her mind could wonder why.

Quick as a blink, he surged closer, hand out as if to steady her, but stopped when she took an unsteady step back.

Disappointment clashed with concern across his face, and something else she couldn't put her finger on. Regret?

Well, so what? Too late for sorry. It didn't change the past or kill the pain.

"It's good to see you." He cleared his throat when she didn't nod or agree.

He took a deliberate step back from her and aimed a slow thumb behind him. Same thumb that used to swipe away her tears and tilt her chin up for good-night kisses. Memories brought warmth to her cheeks.

"I'm going to check on the others." He nodded toward a group of elderly women. "I'll have one of my teammates direct you to an ambulance."

She nodded.

He motioned toward her hand. "You need to have those bones X-rayed and set. Of course, being a doctor, I imagine you know that." He met her gaze and held it like his strong arms had the children going up the hoist rope.

Her mind flashed back ten years ago, to the day he left on a bus to Air Force boot camp. It had taken every ounce of strength not to chase it down the street. While her heart had cried for him to come back, her feet had stayed firmly planted because he'd promised to write every week. In the midst of a heart raging with titanic emotions, her mind and common sense reasoned that he'd enlisted and legally there'd been no getting out of it.

But months later after no letters, her bleeding heart had won, convincing her mind that Nolan had left for something better. Just like her dad had left her mom and Mandy. A better life and she wasn't part of it.

And she'd felt no less abandoned by Nolan. Especially after all the loneliness, emotional trauma and family tumult he'd helped her through. Doing what he was meant to: rescue. He was doing that now but he'd always shown tendencies.

But she wasn't that needy person anymore. She clenched trembling fingers against her side as well as her injuries allowed. All the while he gauged her as though searching for signs of life.

Or lack of.

She dipped her head toward other victims. "Go on. I understand triage. And I'm not *that* hurt."

His chin lifted and his expression took on a knowing manner, as if he'd picked up on the terse tones of the last sentence.

He pivoted, not seeming to be able to remove his gaze. His mouth moved as if to say something.

Slowly, he walked backward as though seeing her was like witnessing someone dead coming back to life.

Yet there resided a deep pain in his eyes that also looked like he'd just seen someone die who'd previously lived.

"Glad to see you're okay, Mandy." His voice sounded unmistakably thick as his eyes, genuine and reminiscently tender, canvassed the dark, swirling water.

At her reply of silence, his wide shoulders drooped as if weighted with something that wasn't pressing on them before he'd seen her. Slowly, he turned.

And then he was gone. Just like that.

And Mandy could not breathe. Could not think. Could not slow her pulse or still her thoughts from reeling or stop her heart from squeezing. Or keep herself from thinking of chasing after him with all her might.

Again.

Chapter Three

"What's up, bro?" Brock clapped a hand on Nolan's shoulder.

Vince hawk-eyed him. "Yeah. Look like you've seen a ghost."

Nolan swallowed. "Feel like I have."

Petrowski looked up. "Don't tell me. You just saw that woman you always used to talk about."

Brock leaned in. "You mean the one he never got over? The reason he won't go on dates, least not second ones?"

Nolan tensed his jaw and gave a slight nod.

"No way!" Vince stood and eyed Mandy from afar.

"Dude! Seriously?" Brock's eyes widened.

"Yeah."

Chance eyed the lot over Nolan's shoulder. "That her?"

Nolan nodded, turning with his team and commander to watch Mandy.

Joy and sadness played ring-around-the-rosy with his heart as he watched her interact with the children and tend their scrapes and bumps despite her injury.

Chance moved to stand next to Nolan. "Didn't y'all part ways so she could go to med school when you joined the military?"

"Yeah."

Petrowski pivoted. "As natural and calm as she was with those children back there, obviously she realized her dream."

Nodding, Nolan pulled out his beret and settled it on his head.

"At the expense of your relationship, though," Brock said.

"I encouraged her to go. At the time I couldn't have offered her as much as medical school." Nolan shrugged, but the niggling feeling of failing Mandy and the hard goodbye they'd had the day he left wouldn't recede. "She'd have lost her funding had I not kept up my end of the bargain." Had he fought for what he wanted—made a way for him and Mandy to be together— her dreams would have been flushed down the drain by those in authority, who wanted nothing more than Nolan away from her.

To get in their way would have resulted in Mandy losing her chance to do the one thing she'd always dreamed: help salvage the lives of children.

As she'd done amazingly today with outstanding bravery and grit.

"What I did was for the best. For both of us." Now whom was he trying to convince? Needing a moment of space, Nolan stepped away from his closest friends and eyed the horizon where purple streaked into pink above the bridge that sat cockeyed over Refuge River. In fact…

Reunion Bridge. The hair on Nolan's neck and arms prickled. No coincidence. God had meant them to meet again. Why?

And why when he was in the midst of having to use every bit of time and energy to be proactive at finding a way out of being taken from his team? And from Refuge, a town he'd come to love. And now from Mandy, right when they'd reunited. Nolan wished Joel was here. And Manny. They'd help him make sense of it all.

He could look to Petrowski, but Aaron was in the same boat as Nolan and then some. Aaron—a single dad and trying to be there for his little boys and his "big" ones, the Pararescue team.

No, Nolan couldn't burden Petrowski further. He'd find a way on his own and trust in God's help.

One by one, the guys knuckled his shoulders and cupped hands on his back, then turned as a unit and started walking off.

Nolan took a step to follow, then turned back. Unable to leave or even look away just yet.

"Ready, Briggs? Or you gonna stand here and gawk at that gorgeous doctor all day?" Petrowski said moments later.

"Gorgeous is right." Mandy had always been pretty. But this woman Mandy had grown into could kick any guy's testosterone into high gear. And his pulse. Yeah. Definitely his pulse.

One more moment. He'd linger. He'd look. But the more he looked, the more he couldn't look away. His heart had hoisted to her the moment he'd seen her again. And heard her voice. And looked into her mesmerizing cat-shaped eyes. Shimmery green. Like sleek, waxen southern Illinois soybean fields.

Eyes that still held a decade-old hurt.

Memories he'd forgotten assaulted him in waves as he remembered all they'd shared.

He faced Petrowski. "Even before we were sweethearts, we were inseparable growing up. Neighborhood buddies. Confidants." Nolan smiled, recalling a particular blackberry bush burglary. "Partners in crime at times. Best friends."

Soul mates.

The thought shook something loose. A determination he didn't know he possessed blasted forth. He lifted his binoculars, aimed her way.

An unseen pressure moved them back down.

Chance grinned. "Dude, that borders on stalking."

Nolan lowered the binoculars and tucked them away, wishing he could do the same with the film of memories reeling through his mind right now.

"You still have a thing for her?" Vince reached for the binoculars. "Lemme see why."

Nolan laughed and knocked away his hand. "Not on your life."

"You two have a history." Petrowski's world-wise eyes smiled. "Strange you'd meet again. Here. This way."

"What kinda history?" Brock waggled his reddish brows.

Nolan shook his head. "Not *that* kind. She was a good girl." *Who fell for the bad boy.* At least that's what Mandy's mother and her pastor claimed. Their influence had been like a tumor in his and Mandy's relationship, metastasizing it with the poison of pious principles.

Nolan hadn't shared Mandy's family's faith. Therefore she was off-limits, according to them and the Bible they quoted. The book he'd wanted nothing to do with because he feared it would judge him as harshly and unmercifully as they did.

Now, as a new Christian, he understood completely. But at the time, their judgmental precepts had incited and incised him.

"Where are they transporting?" Nolan asked Petrowski and forced his feet to move. He observed a Red Cross volunteer finishing up paperwork with Mandy and directing her to the far end of the parking lot with waiting ambulances.

"Refuge Memorial for now. Completely swamped from so many bridge victims being brought in. So patients will be diverted elsewhere."

Nolan shucked off his jumpsuit, glad he'd worn jeans and a T-shirt beneath. "So all injured are being taken there initially?"

Zips sounded as Aaron shirked his own suit. "Far as I know."

"I can go talk with her there. We never had proper closure." Nolan wadded his suit and tossed it in his rucksack.

Aaron tilted his head. "And, according to her response back there, you *need* to."

"Exactly right." He couldn't let this go. Not again. He didn't realize the impact of that open wound until the moment they'd laid eyes on one another after a decade of zero contact.

They needed to talk, if nothing more than to ease shut the chapter of a very painful book. He'd seen it in her eyes.

He'd hurt her. Majorly wronged her.

And he needed to make it right.

"How rude," Mandy muttered to herself as she stepped away from the volunteer, and Nolan's scrutiny. Ow, did her hand hurt. Starting to swell, too. A blue-black discoloration had begun. Hand elevated, she trudged toward the distant line of ambulances she'd been directed to. Maybe they'd have pain relievers on board. And another ice pack. To cool off her wrist.

And her temper.

Nolan and his friends had been openly staring and talking about her. Without trying to hide it. What kind of friends did he have nowadays? She couldn't hear what they said but knew for certain she was the object of conversation.

And she had felt Nolan's stare above the rest.

Where was he?

She started to look around but stopped herself. She'd jump off the bridge before she'd broadcast how badly he'd rattled her. He had to be tracking her. She could still perceive him. Right now. Gaze drilled into her back right to her heart.

No matter.

This freakish accident tumbled them together but she wasn't about to make anything out of it. He'd better not follow her to the hospital, either. She had nothing to say to him. Nothing.

Never mind small pings of joy that he would actually make an effort to come see her. Why would he?

The cold, sharp truth smarted like a dull needle. She hadn't meant enough to him ten years ago or he would have found a way.

And she would not risk her heart to a man like that again. She'd have to mean more to him than his dreams.

To be fair, she hadn't considered giving up hers, either.

Couldn't have expected Nolan to give up his. He really hadn't had a choice whereas she had but hadn't taken it.

Seeing how he rescued people today made her glad he hadn't. The world needed men like that, willing to risk their lives so others can live. Their relationship had been a casualty of his creed and her cause.

She was no longer on his radar. Not even close. No use hoping for a relationship that had ended a decade ago.

Sweat trickled down Mandy's back as she continued her trek across asphalt so hot it probably melted the tread on her soles. An EMT approached. "Think you can ride sitting up, Dr. Manchester?" he asked as she reached the line of open-door ambulances that had come from towns around to assist.

"Yes."

Reece, Caden and Jayna sat like three lost baby ducks in a row inside a middle ambulance. The urge to shelter them hit her. How she loved children. She had an especially tender heart for fragile ones. She nodded that way. "If there's room in there, I'll ride with them."

"Sure. But might be a bit before transport since we may need to stick a couple others in it." He eyed her injuries.

Mandy nodded. "That's fine."

Hand lent, the EMT assisted her inside, and closed the door.

"Miss Mandy!" Reece scooted over and patted a place beside her. Bless the child's assessment that her bottom could actually fit in that small space.

Caden must have noticed Mandy's dilemma. He unlatched the strap across his thighs and moved to the bench.

"Scoot an itty bit more," Mandy said, then sat between Reece and Jayna.

Grinning, Reece fisted her hand and lifted it to Mandy.

She smiled. "Just what am I supposed to do with that?"

Jayna giggled. "You go like this." She fisted her hand and bumped Reece's knuckles.

"Hi-fives aren't hip anymore?"

Caden scowled. "No way. Neither is 'hip.' It's older'n my grandma's dinosaur's grandma."

Reece and Jayna erupted in giggles and squashed themselves up against her.

"Hey, Caden, I never did catch your last name." Mandy wiggled her nose at the little boy.

"Boyle," he said. Mandy caught sight of Nolan walking past. Looking for something? Someone? Her heart slammed against her sternum when he passed by, then disappeared from sight.

God, I miss him. Hurts too much to hope…

Mandy consciously repressed it all.

"Chief Boyle…" Mandy tilted her face in a dreamy lilt, making pretense of eyeing the ceiling, while actually looking for emergency items. Habit she supposed. "I do believe I like the sound of that."

The children chortled.

Mandy joined them and felt the unprecedented stress of an unbearably hard day melt away. "Well all-right-y then. Fist bumps are what people do nowadays." She raised hers and bumped each child, causing bubbly giggles to fill the ambulance.

The door opened and the EMT poked his head inside. "Dr. Manchester, you well enough to be the transport medic if I stay and ready other patients for air evacuation?"

"Absolutely. I'm right in my element here." She smiled.

So did the EMT. "Any questions on where stuff is?"

She looked around, catching sight of the most important things. Oxygen. IV equipment. Code meds, though none of these children would need any of that. She searched for a seatbelt for the booth. "How do I secure them in?"

The EMT whose nametag read "Cole" tugged a clasp from a crack between padded benches. "Any other questions?"

"Why yes, in fact I do. Did you know fist bumps are in and hi-fives are old news?"

Cole laughed. "I'd heard fist bumps were a wave of the future." He lifted his hand and touched gentle knuckles to each child, then Mandy's. "Thank you." He cast a deeply thankful look to her and closed the door.

Past him, through the windows, she could see men dressed as Nolan had been, assisting other paramedics with stabilizing those who would be flown to other hospitals. Probably those specializing in head and spinal trauma. The thought made her want to leap from the ambulance and help her fellow medical workers.

Likewise, the thought that Nolan, though unseen, could be on the other side of the doors made her want to bolt out and see him. Hold him. Catch up. Connect. Recapture something, anything. The sensation of being the only person in the world who knew the other so profoundly. They'd had a bond like nothing she'd ever known.

Then, one day, nothing.

Hands fisted, Mandy pressed them beneath her thighs and tilted toward the children. "So, what was your field trip?" The bus driver had explained it was an end-of-the-year gig but hadn't said where. Chitchat would keep the kids' minds off missing their parents, and her mind off missing Nolan.

Reece grinned. "We went to a science museum. It was fun."

As the children chattered on, Mandy stacked pillows under her elbow and leaned back. Her wrist throbbed like crazy. But she didn't want to trouble Cole or any others for pain meds. From some of the serious injuries she'd passed on her way to the ambulance, she definitely sat at the bottom of the triage totem.

Through the windows, a tawny-haired man with a military buzz came back into view. She didn't have to strain her eyes to know it was Nolan. Nor did she have to see his eyes to know they were the most brilliant shade of blue.

As if sensing her stare, he shifted and looked around. She stiffened, then relaxed and craned her neck. He couldn't know she was in this ambulance. Nor that she could watch him unaware. She could only see him from the shoulders up, and he was totally out of sight of the children, who would undoubtedly bombard her with questions should they notice her noticing Nolan.

He conversed with someone she couldn't see, but his gaze kept coming back to sweep the line of ambulances.

She grew enthralled watching him. The lithe motions. Firm jaw. That lopsided grin that had graced her almost daily growing up as he'd walked her home from school because they lived in a bad neighborhood. The familiar yet now mature animation on his face elicited a sense of loneliness that made her miss him.

He bent and lifted something, probably a patient. He looked utterly in his element. Like he was born to do this.

Just like you were born to be a doctor.

Unfortunately their dreams were like two strong arms tugging them apart and in opposite directions. Yet they'd championed one another's hopes and goals practically since the day they met.

IV bag in hand, Nolan shifted something and raised his arm.

"Miss Mandy, why do we gotta go to the hospital if we aren't hurt?" Caden asked, breaking the bittersweet trance.

Metal clanked together as Mandy secured a seatbelt over him. "Because that's where they're telling your parents to come pick you up. And because the doctors and nurses will want to check you out and make sure you didn't get any bumps and bruises that might need Band-Aids."

He nodded. "Miss Mandy, do you have any Band-Aids?"

She spread fingers on her good hand. "Sadly, I'm fresh out. But the nice doctors and nurses at the hospital will have Band-Aids and stickers. Maybe even lollipops. How about that?"

Mandy laughed.

"What's so funny?" Reece asked.

"Just thinking about how nurses give the shots and doctors give the lollipops." Mandy wiggled her nose at Reece, who grinned. "But my office will be different." She might call the shots and have her nurses give them, but she'd let them also dole out stickers.

Nolan moved from her line of sight. The air inside the ambulance vacuumed all hers in a sudden panic. She resisted the urge to push open the door.

Focus. Focus on the children. Forget about Nolan. Focus.

Caden grinned, revealing lost teeth. "I wanted the Band-aids for Bearby. Looks like he could fall apart."

Reece clutched the brown bear appendage to her. "He does not! It's just that his fur falls out because I love on him so much." She sent a harsh scowl at Caden.

He blinked at her like she was an alien. Then tilted his face up. "Miss Mandy, why do you want to be a doctor? Our teacher says it takes lots of school. School's boring."

Mandy chuckled as she brushed a hand along Bearby's disheveled fur and contemplated the question.

Jayna leaned her head against Mandy's side and hugged her arm. "You were right, Miss Mandy. They came for us."

"And got us all off," Caden said. "Every single one."

Mandy forced a calm, convincing smile. These precious children did not need to know that not everyone had made it off the bridge or out of the water alive. As sure as she lived, she would take those horrific images of the collapse to her own grave.

Reece leaned close to Mandy's other side. "And you kept us not afraid anymore. Thank you." She pressed her stuffed animal's ebony nose to her ear. "What? Oh." She turned his smooshed-in face toward her ribs, like the toy was being shy. She leaned in and whispered, "Bearby says he thinks he loves you."

Emotion lodged words in Mandy's throat. She'd noticed Reece projecting thoughts and emotions onto the toy earlier.

Mandy couldn't have spoken if she'd wanted. So she smiled. Deeply, at each little expectant face.

This is why. These children. This feeling of accomplishment and knowing she could make a difference in the life of a child and their family in a difficult season.

She wrapped an arm around the two girls, and reached over to bump a gentle fingertip playfully on Caden's nose.

"Children like you are why I do what I do."

Leaning in, Mandy knuckled her hand and lightly fist-bumped Bearby's tattered paw. "And for the record, Bearby, I think I love you, too."

Chapter Four

"Mommy! That's Miss Mandy, the nice doctor lady who helped us," a familiar voice pealed through the hospital corridor.

Mandy rose from her chair in the hallway outside the bustling Refuge E.R. waiting room. She smiled at the woman walking toward her with Reece and her stuffed bear in tow.

"C'mon!" Reece tucked Bearby beneath her arm and dragged her mother faster.

Upon approach, deep gratitude glistened from the young woman's eyes. Uncanny how much she looked like an older version of Reece.

The woman breached the space between them like a close family member would and grasped Mandy's uninjured hand. "I'm Amelia North, Reece's mom."

"I'm Dr. Manchester. Please call me Mandy."

"Thank you for watching over our children on the bridge." Amelia's grip tightened when the words strained from her throat. The heartfelt tone put a sting to Mandy's eyes. What's with that? She hadn't cried since she was a teen.

"I'm thankful they weren't hurt. Truth is, they kept me brave." It wasn't a lie. Being responsible for them had lessened her fear and panic.

Reece plopped onto a chair. She danced Bearby on her knees.

"That couldn't have been easy with you being injured." Amelia eyed Mandy's splint. "How did you stay strong for them?"

"Imagined myself in a parent's place. Kept in mind they were depending on me. Acted as I'd want mine treated if I had any." Mandy brushed fingers through Reece's curls.

"You're not a mommy?" Reece wiggled close to Mandy's lap.

She leaned eye level. "Not yet."

Reece lifted her comfort toy. "Bearby wants to know why not."

Mandy faced Bearby. "I still have some doctor training left so I can learn how to take the best care of people." She started to add that she'd also like to find a husband first, but the words caught in her throat.

She discreetly eyed Amelia's left hand. A heart-shaped diamond winked back, but no wedding band. Gaze averted, her mind zeroed in on Reece. Thankfully Mandy hadn't said anything. Wasn't her place to judge or wonder about the situation.

"Bearby thinks you'll make a good doctor, and a good mommy." Making engine noises, Reece puttered Bearby in the air.

Mandy tilted her head. "Thank you. On both counts."

"Is your hand in terrible pain?" Amelia set her purse on the chair beside her near the E.R. waiting room door.

TVs blared from different stations, all filled with images of the collapse. Her chest hurt at the sights playing out. Mandy turned away. But she could still hear the announcer describing the ordeal. Sweat broke out over Mandy's brow. She tried to dab it but her arms felt robotic and numb.

Concern flashed across Amelia's face. "Are you okay?"

Mandy stood on legs that felt as rubbery as the business end of a reflex hammer. As quickly as possible, she turned the

TV volume down, ignoring caustic looks from waiting room patrons. "I am now," she said to Amelia as she returned to the seat beside her.

The smells of antiseptic and sickness hung in the air. Call lights rang down the halls, and a hacking cough emerged from the room beside her that made Mandy want to whip out a prescription pad.

Reece peeped at the temporary splint Nolan had applied.

"Is it broken?" Reece blinked up at her.

Hesitation hovered inside Mandy's thoughts. She wanted to be honest yet tread lightly. "I think so, but no one's looked at it yet. They're taking care of the worst injured first."

"How will they tell?" Reece asked.

"They'll take special pictures called X-rays."

"Will they hurt?"

"If they have to straighten out my hand it might. Otherwise, X-rays usually don't hurt at all." She smiled at Reece.

"Mommy could go with you and hold your hand. She's good at that. She holds my hand when I get shots. And you could hug Bearby during it. He makes people brave."

"He sure does." Mandy kneaded Bearby's fuzzy mis-shapen head.

"Then him and Mommy will go with you." Reece's expression declared the matter settled.

Amelia fingered Reece's curly brown hair. "I'm sure Dr. Manchester has someone who can sit with her."

Mandy shifted uncomfortably. In the confusion, she had left her purse which contained her cell phone, in her car on the bridge. An officer had left a message with the nurses' desk saying he'd recovered it and would bring it by when he had a moment. Not that she had anyone here she could call once she had it. Miss Ivy didn't drive.

Perceptive awareness entered Amelia's eyes. "Need to

borrow my phone to call someone?" She pulled her purse onto her lap and extracted a cell phone.

Heat of a blush crept over Mandy. "No, I'll be all right. Besides, I'm fairly new in town and really don't know anyone. My mother lives in a different state."

Called Oblivion.

"Would you like us to sit with you while you wait?" Amelia tucked her phone back in her purse.

"No, it's fine." But a thought struck her. Who would take her home? She'd be unable to drive herself if she took pain medication or if she had a sling on her arm. "Does Refuge have a cab service?"

"No. Small town. We could give you a ride if they let you go."

"I'd hate to make you wait. I imagine it will be past Reece's bedtime before staff get to me."

"It won't hurt her to get to bed late one night." She gave Reece's ponytail an affectionate tug. "Will it?"

Mischief alive in her eyes, Reece grinned like she'd just gotten away with something big. "I *like* staying up late!"

Mandy and Amelia laughed.

"We live at the Refuge Bed and Breakfast on the edge of town. It only takes thirty minutes to get here," Amelia said.

Mandy shifted. "I don't know…" Thirty minutes there, then here then to Mandy's and back would take at least two hours out of Reece's sleep time.

Despite Mandy's hesitation, Amelia handed her a card. "Here are my numbers. I doubt they'll have school tomorrow with what's happened." *With what's happened.*

Knowing she meant the bridge collapse, Mandy studied the chic business card to block horrific images that threatened in her mind's eyes. "You do caricature art?"

"In my spare time. I also manage Refuge's B and B. Promise you'll call if you need a ride?"

Suddenly, she didn't feel embarrassed about being needy. "I will."

"Maybe we can meet for coffee next week, too?" Amelia asked.

"I'd love that."

Her face lit up. "Say goodbye, Reece."

"Bye, Miss Mandy. I don't like how we had to meet but I'm glad we did. So is Bearby." Reece hugged Mandy.

Mandy reciprocated the hug. "I'm glad we met, too. I'm glad you weren't hurt."

"Or lost in the scary water." Reece took hold of her mom's hand. "Mommy would have been so sad."

Mandy's heart pounded with memories of watching cars in front of her plunge into the depths of Refuge River. Her hands trembled and so did her lips. Sounds from the wreck clanged in her ears and drowned out rational thought. She drew deep breaths and focused on Reece's antics with Bearby until the impending flashback receded. She rubbed sudden moisture off her quaking palm by running it across her thigh. "I don't blame her. I would have been sad, too. But you are safe—and you are here."

But others weren't.

Mandy fought debilitating dread at the grief and hardship that families of those who didn't get out of their cars in time were going through this instant. Several survivors were permanently injured, which was why it was taking so long for her to be seen. "If there was a room or even equipment free, I'd go back there and treat myself."

Amelia laughed. "You're gutsier than me."

"I seriously would, just to ease the staff's burden and relieve someone of duty. The hospital is on trauma alert. Every available space is taken. And my injuries are minor."

"Couldn't waiting be bad for you if it's broken?" Amelia eyed her wrist with concern.

Mandy shrugged, not wanting to think about things like nerve damage from swelling and how that would affect her work.

"What does a broken bone feel like, Miss Mandy?" Reece asked.

"Like it got hit." *With a sledgehammer. Hard. Twenty times*.

"Owie." Reece nuzzled Mandy's sling with Bearby.

"Ah-ah-ah." Amelia guided the bear away. "We don't touch."

"Bearby's just trying to make Miss Mandy feel better. Hospitals are scary." Reece darted wide eyes around, then scooted closer to Amelia.

She's afraid. Mandy felt bad for them staying here on her account. "I work in hospitals all the time. I'll be fine if you'd like to go home."

"Can we, Mommy? I love Miss Mandy but I'm scared."

"Sure." Amelia held Reece and cast Mandy apologetic glances.

"It's fine. Honestly. I will call you if I need something."

"Okay. Would it be an imposition to get your phone number so I can check on you? And verify you're still up for coffee?"

"Not at all. You have paper and something to write with?"

Amelia pulled out a notebook with an attached mini pen.

Mandy scribbled as best she could left-handed. "Here you go."

"I won't share this info with anyone."

Mandy laughed. "Didn't think you would. No one ever calls me anyway. Not even telemarketers." *No one ever calls me*.

Why had she revealed that? Especially when bursts of sympathy spritzed from Amelia's eyes? No one needed to burden themselves with her loneliness. Yet something about Amelia North beckoned. She emanated warmth and trust conducive to friendship.

"Be glad about the telemarketers. We get calls all day long." Laughing, Amelia picked up Reece. "Let's skedaddle so Miss Mandy can rest." They made their way to the exit.

Mandy missed the company immediately. The chatter had kept her mind off the pain. She closed her eyes to mentally wash it out but instead, images of water swirling through broken car windows rushed in.

She jerked open her eyes and sat up. Sweat broke out over her cheeks, forehead and palms. Whether from the flashback or the pain, she couldn't be sure.

A hand rested on her shoulder. She looked up.

"Dr. Manchester?" Nurse Bailey hovered. "How're you faring?"

Mandy tilted her good hand sideways and back. "Hanging in."

"It's gonna be another couple hours before someone can set that fracture. All the docs are in surgery. Sure you don't wanna pain shot?" Her face revealed empathetic apology.

"I'm sure." She'd never had narcotics and didn't want to lose control in front of staff. "I can wait."

Nurse Bailey looked doubtful. "All right then. Call me if you change your mind."

The more Mandy watched her coworkers, nurses and other medical personnel scurry about, the more restless she became.

She blew out a frustrated breath. Feeling a snooze coming on, she leaned her head against the wall and closed her eyes.

Warmth spread across her stomach, arms and chest. She stretched open her eyes. Sound trickled into her consciousness. Someone stood above her. Someone familiar. She blinked awake.

"Nolan?" Her heart began to pound and she reached for him. Then remembered.

She tucked her hands back beneath the gauzy white hospital blanket he must have brought and spread out over her torso.

"Hey." He knelt in front of her. "You haven't been seen yet?"

She shook her head. "They're swamped."

"How are you holding up?" He tugged the blanket back and

palpated her fingers, peeking through the stretchy bandage he'd applied on the bridge.

"Fair."

"It's twice as swollen as on the bridge. What did they give you for pain?"

Her voice caught at the softness in his. "I—I haven't had anything." She dipped her face, partly to avoid the compassion in his. How she hated to be weak in front of him again.

Nolan rose, looking determinedly down halls, probably for a nurse.

Mandy straightened. "They offered but I declined it."

He inclined his head. "Now why would you go and do a silly—"

"Dr. Manchester?" Nurse Bailey approached.

Thank goodness. Saved by the Bailey.

"Yes?" Mandy stood.

Nolan stepped back but put his hand to her unaffected elbow.

Bailey motioned toward the unit. "You're up next. Come on back."

Nolan made motions to follow. Mandy held her hand palm up in halt position. Comically annoyed but steadfast, he looked at it like it was no barrier. When his gaze reached hers, he stopped and drew a long breath that made his chest bigger. Like it needed it. Not!

"Look Mandy, I came here to see how you were. But also, I wanted to set up a time to meet. We need to talk."

Her hand jammed to her hip. "Not interested in discussing anything." Knees trembling, she turned to go.

A strong hand curled around her healthy wrist. "Don't be mule-headed." He moved toward the room with her still in hand.

She stopped, tugged her hand free and shot him a caustic glare. "Bye, Nolan."

His body tensed, but paused. The knot in his jaw rippled.

Always a sign of frustration in Nolan. Yet rarely, if ever, had it been directed at her.

She turned to go to the room Nurse Bailey disappeared into.

"This is far from over, Mandy." The decree floated from somewhere behind her.

She ignored him until she reached the room entrance. Then mistakenly cast a glance over her shoulder to see if he'd actually listened to her and left.

Right.

He stood, stubborn and tall, feet planted right where her words had left him. And according to the steel-plated glint in his resolute eyes he not only wasn't going anywhere, her words may as well have fallen on deaf ears.

He wasn't budging.

This is far from over.

Then an unspoken version of that message traveled, mesmerizingly slow and daringly potent, down the corridor from his eyes to hers. And his immovable jutting stance said exactly the same yet fractionally different:

We are far from over.

Chapter Five

"It's broken for sure?" Mandy askd Dr. Riviera after she'd been taken to a room and her wrist X-rayed.

"Yes."

A sinking feeling hit her gut. "Are soft tissues involved?"

Wheels on the med cart squeaked as he pushed it toward her. "Subsequent X-rays and an MRI will tell for sure. But judging by the pain, swelling and disfigured angle of the hand, I'm guessing yes."

"Figured as much." How would this affect her job? Could she safely carry out examinations with her left hand when she was right-handed? Her mind clicked through common procedures. Discouragement abounded.

A knock sounded at the door. "Bailey in here?" a male voice Mandy recognized as Dr. Callahan's asked. "We have issues in nine and could use another pair of arms."

"You're in hot demand today." Mandy smiled at Bailey, feeling compassion for the tired woman. All the wrung-out staff, really.

"Always. Excuse me." Nurse Bailey scurried out.

Dr. Riviera suddenly looked weary as he moved into the

light. Dark shadows circled his normally bright eyes, now blood-shot. Puffy bags of skin clung to them, making him look older.

Empathy filled her. "You've been here all night?"

He nodded and offered a tired smile. "I'll get relief soon. I wanted to see your treatment through first." He stifled a yawn.

"I understand." She eyed the cart and moved to the edge of the table's padded seat. Paper crinkled beneath her. "So what torture are you about to inflict, hmm?"

He chuckled. "First, I need to know how you're getting home. If these bones aren't aligned, we'll need to reset the hand."

Ouch. "I know."

"Which means you also know I'll have to heavily sedate or anesthetize you?"

She gritted her teeth and nodded.

He unwrapped her bandage. "Whoever splinted this did a fabulous job."

Mandy licked her lips and stared at a spot on the wall.

"Be right back and we'll get this fixed up after I snag someone to help me. Now that Callahan stole Bailey from me."

It took longer than Mandy expected for the door to open. Dr. Riviera re-entered, armed with hot pink casting paraphernalia.

Bailey started Mandy's IV, then left to answer a call light.

Wheels creaked as an anesthetist entered with a cart. "You're not going to be able to walk home after we apply this." He looked pointedly at Mandy's wrist, the anesthesia cart and casting material. "Is there someone you can call?"

"I'd offer a ride but we have a mandatory stress debriefing," Riviera said.

"I imagine patients need this bed, too." Occupied gurneys crammed all hallways with curtained partitions around them. Guilt slammed her over having this private room.

"Other than you and Doc Callahan, the two hoodlums who recruited me to supposedly calm Refuge, I don't know anyone awake at this hour." She hated to wake Amelia.

"You know me," Nolan said from the door.

Her head lifted.

He must have had a shower because he looked clean-shaven and wore civilian clothes. Trendy jeans hugged lean legs, revealing muscles she hadn't noticed yesterday. His shirt caught her attention too. A pressed black button up with silvery-white pin stripes—her favorite colors. Coincidence? Or did he remember? Nolan never wore black in the summer.

She cleared her throat and eyed her supervisor.

Dr. Riviera watched them with amused interest.

"May I come in?" Nolan asked.

Mandy shifted. "Looks like you already are."

Guilt prodded Mandy to squirm under his gently inquisitive eyes.

Vague recollections of him walking her to the lab and imaging departments last night seeped into her thoughts. Holding her as she'd tried not to yelp from pain as technicians straightened her hand to get a good image. He'd talked her through the procedure as a doula coached a woman through labor. Like he'd talked her through hundreds of problems growing up.

And, because meds had lowered her resistance, she'd let him.

"I'm not really up for visitors, Nolan."

"How's it going, Airman Briggs?" Ignoring her, Dr. Riviera walked to the door and extended his hand. "Nice job on the bridge. Got all the children off safely, I hear."

"Yeah, thanks." Nolan shook Riviera's hand.

"Rumor has it you might be leaving soon?" Riviera said.

Mandy looked up. What? Leaving? What?

Nolan's jaw tensed. "Maybe."

"How soon?"

"In a few months unless plan D works."

Plan D? If they'd gone through plans A, B and C, that

wasn't good, right? Why would he be leaving? She'd asked Cole about the PJs and he'd informed them the pararescue team was stationed in Refuge since it sat on the edge of Eagle Point Air Base.

"I hope it does. I hate to see you go," Riviera said.

"Yeah. Me, too." Nolan faced Mandy. He marched in like a warrior on a mission. "Look, we need to talk. Besides, you could use a distraction for when they treat those injuries." He nodded at her wrist, elevated and wrapped in ice.

True. She did.

She eyed Dr. Riviera. His head lowered the way it did when he administered verbal pop quizzes to residents. "And I could use his help. Bailey bailed on me."

She couldn't very well make herself out to look like a hag in front of the head of her medical department, now could she?

Mandy gritted her teeth and nodded toward a chair near where the anesthetist readied equipment. "Come on in then, Nolan." Get this over with and *leave.*

Since you're so good at it.

"Thanks." He didn't take the chair. He took the spot right beside her and leaned against the exam table.

Dr. Riviera approached with a fresh hand splint. "Nurses are stretched beyond human limit. So I'm going to have Airman Briggs, who is essentially a paramedic, assist me. You okay with that, Dr. Manchester? It'll be good training."

For what, emotional torture?

What could she do except nod?

Dr. Riviera's pager went off. He peered at it. "Be right back." He slipped from the room. She could have sworn she saw the hint of a smile as he went out the door, too. The anesthesiologist followed.

Utter conspiracy.

Putrid doctors.

Nolan rested a hand on her elbow. She tried not to flinch.

Hated that she could feel his breath against her neck and hair as he leaned over. "Look, I'm sorry about that. I just wanted a chance to talk. Didn't know he was going to draft me into helping with your procedures. You okay with that?"

Mandy held his gaze as long as she could without being rattled. And knew she couldn't be a ninny about this. She stood from the table and walked across the room. "I trust you, Nolan. At least medically. I saw what you did on that bridge."

The amazing things.

Someone knocked. "Miss Manchester?"

"Yes?"

"Officer Stallings. I have something you might need."

"Please come in."

The striking officer stepped around the corner with a dashing grin and her purse.

"Oh! You found it. Thank you!"

He handed it over with a little nod of his head. Man, did he have dimples-to-die-for or what? Yet he paled in comparison to Nolan. At least in her estimation. "Best contact your insurance company about your car as soon as possible, ma'am."

Sweet southern manners and a delightful drawl to boot. She took the purse. "I will. Thank you."

"Bye, now." He tipped his hat and turned to go. "Briggs." The officer nodded at Nolan on his way out.

Nolan gave a stiff nod back. "Stallings."

"That came out terse," Mandy said after the officer left.

"What?"

She puffed out her chest and tilted her chin in exaggerated motions. Then lowered her voice to majorly male octaves. "'Briggs.' 'Stallings.'"

Nolan's eyes smiled. "You're imagining things." His arms crossed, causing a heap of muscles to strain against his shirt. It couldn't hide the massive chest. Concrete arms. Flat stomach. Not an ounce of fat anywhere.

She swayed away before admiration at how hard he must have worked to get himself to this place of extreme physical fortitude could cart her away.

Fighting adoration, she sniffed. "He's cute." *Though not as cute as you.*

"Who? Stallings?" Nolan's arms lowered to his sides. But his hands were fisted, she noticed.

She pretended to study the view from the window. "Yep."

"That supposed to make me jealous, Mandy?"

She whirled. "I don't know. Is it?"

He creased his arms again, but remained silent.

Feet squaring off with his, she flipped hair that had lost the battle with the clip over her shoulder. "Well, are you?"

"Am I what?"

"Jealous." She raised one brow.

Showdown. "I don't know. Am I?"

Something in her deflated. "I don't know."

And blast her, she wanted to.

Her feet took her back to the window before nonsense could take hold. She harbored an angry inward groan. Maybe some of it leaked out because Nolan approached. She pivoted away.

Staying in step with her, he swallowed. "You're not very happy to see me. Are you?"

"From a bridge collapse victim's standpoint, and as someone in need of medical attention, yes. I'm very happy to see you." She rubbed her arm.

"But nothing else? Not on a personal level?" Standing side by side, he grazed his pinky along her ring finger.

She half closed her eyelids.

He leaned in, looking at her with penetrating eyes. The way he always did when he knew something tormented her but she wouldn't talk. Until he'd disassembled all barriers of communication.

But she was stronger now. Didn't need him to sort out her troubles. He had no reason to still feel responsible for her. Yet that was just the way with Nolan. Apparently he hadn't grown out of rescue mode.

"Nothing." Straightening to her full height she folded her arms, hoping to send a clear signal that she was no longer weak.

His eyes narrowed. Once again he studied her entire face before gazing deeply into her eyes. "Nothing? Nothing at all?"

She couldn't speak. His hand came forward, skin grazed her neck. He fingered the panda charm. "After all this?"

She resisted the urge to jerk her collar tighter.

She shied away from his reach trying to look poised and squeezed her collar anyway. That way he wouldn't see the black-and-silver beaded chain containing the one thing he'd given her that she couldn't let go of.

A voice blew through her mind like rushing wind.

He gave you more. Courage. Self-confidence. Friendship.

Enough! she ordered back.

His face softened at her jerky motions. "You're trembling."

"I saw a dozen people die yesterday in a horrific bridge collapse that nearly flipped my car hood over bumper. Of course I'm going to have an autonomic response."

What she did not expect was his potent grin that stretched from one ear to the other. "Using doctor-ly words. A sure sign of distress." His mouth closed but still twitched with a smile.

"Not a chance." The nerve of the man! She felt like stomping. Oh! The. Nerve!

"We'll see." He lifted his chin.

So did she. And for the first time in her life, wished she was even taller than her five-foot-ten frame. "No, we won't." If his quirking brows and widening smile were any indication, she didn't need X-ray vision to detect that his thoughts were perfectly aligned with hers. There was still something beating between them. Maybe only a faint pulse, but detectable nonetheless.

"We met again on Reunion Bridge," he added.

"It doesn't mean anything. I drive over it four times a day." *Like I'd like to do to your smirking face.* "In a car. With muddy tires."

His eyebrows crinkled. Then straightened. He shifted to his other foot. "It has to mean something. No coincidence that the bridge is called Reunion."

"The bridge is broken and life was lost."

He shook his head. Slow. Determined. And so methodically it made her want to grind her teeth. "Not all of it."

Mandy gulped.

His eyes softened into a vulnerable invitation, daring her to read it. Explore the possibility of friendship at least. She couldn't deny the bond they'd shared nor stop the memories seeing him had resuscitated.

"Let's see how much damage has been done. Then we can determine how difficult this will be to repair." Dr. Riviera's words as he reentered the room sliced through her like a scalpel in surgery. Both cutting and healing at the same time.

For those innocuous words fit their unspoken situation with surgical precision.

And Mandy knew for certain God had brought her to this place. Not just this hospital, but to a divine kind of surgery. Not just physical. But spiritual.

As a doctor, she knew surgery meant cutting through healthy tissue to reach the broken, damaged and bruised.

Even as a runaway Christian, she knew God spoke in terms with which a person was familiar. She studied Nolan and wondered what being near him would bring. If it would bring her closer to being back in love with him, she was in double trouble. Because his job was obviously apt to take him away. Again. She must guard her heart at all costs.

But as far as the bigger picture…

He was right. Something bigger—*someone* rather—brought them back together. But for what reason?

And what about when their careers took them away again?

In order to move forward, she had to be healed from her past.

Chapter Six

"Airman Briggs, will you still be available to drive her home?" Dr. Riviera asked. "She's certainly in no shape to get herself there."

Mandy shot upright, prepared to argue, but paused when the walls whirled around her. Not only that, Nolan's expression and body language reflected he was fully prepared to meet her protest and win.

She eyed her cast and asked for the umpteenth time, "Are you sure it's not too tight?"

Dr. Riviera examined parts of her fingers protruding. "I'm sure. It's swollen right now. That'll resolve."

"Would that be before or after you have to amputate my fingers from poor circulation?" Mandy adjusted the arm sling.

Dr. Riviera chuckled and faced Nolan. "Doctors make the worst patients."

"How bad does your wrist hurt?" Nolan asked.

"Like someone's stomping on it."

"Are the pain meds not helping?" Dr. Riviera asked.

Mandy gave a sharp laugh. "No, I think they just make me not care that I hurt."

"You might need a stronger dose." Riviera nodded to Bailey who left, then returned with a syringe of pain medication.

"Mandy? Can you stand up for me?"

Again, seeing Nolan brought everything surging back. Anxiety coiled and twisted in her chest, accelerating her heart rate. She put her hand there.

Nolan eyed her with concern. "You okay?

She nodded. "Just feel panicky is all."

"Still prone to anxiety attacks?"

She dropped her gaze, recalling attacks he'd talked her through growing up. "No. Not for years. At least, not until the collapse." She lowered her voice.

When he drew close to help her from a table to a wheelchair, his scent pleased her more than it ought.

She held his sinewy forearm for support. "Wow. Strong stuff. Er, that morphine and Versed." *And iron-man muscles. And that compelling cologne.* "You really ought not to be wearing it."

Mouth twitching, his brows clashed. "Morphine and Versed?"

She fluttered her hands down her face because it felt numb and tingly. And tickly. Like feathers brushed across it. She swiped again but didn't feel anything on her fingers. Strange. "Yes. No. Never mind. I suppose I'm not making any sense."

A choked laugh. "Not a bit. In fact, it reminds me of the time I swung you around so fast on the tire swing you passed out. Remember that?" Gentle nostalgia coated his face, as if he willed her to remember.

The innocent sweetheart image lodged itself in her brain and proceeded to melt her insides.

"I remember." Despite not wanting to, Mandy smiled at the memory of Nolan running her into the house yelling for help. "Mom was so entirely livid."

"So, how is your mom, Mandy?" As hostile as Mandy's mom had been to Nolan, his question seemed shockingly sincere.

She shrugged, evading the subject of her mother at all costs. "Don't talk to her much."

Nolan's motions slowed to a pause, then resumed.

Mandy blinked her eyes to focus.

His arm tightened around her waist. "Everything feel like it's going in slow motion?"

"Yeah. Including me. Whew."

He chuckled. The sound tried to implant itself in a place she'd kept closed off since the day she figured out he wasn't going to contact her. Old hurt tried to rear its ugly head.

Mandy's cell phone rang. The ID said Amelia was calling. A sudden cheerfulness accosted Mandy. "Hey," she answered.

"Hey. You sound chipper."

"I am." She eyed Nolan, who stepped from the room. She didn't want to admit he was part of the reason. But he was.

"How ya feelin?"

"Better. Tell Reece she'd be proud of me. I chose a hot pink cast, just for her. No rhinestones though."

Another pleasant laugh drifted through the phone. "I called to see how you were and if you need a ride or anything."

"I have a ride, actually. But I will call you later. Maybe you can drop by for a visit in the next few days. I'll undoubtedly get bored. And I love company." And she really did want to get to know Amelia better. She sensed friendship on the horizon.

"Sounds great. Reece is about to have a high-speed freakout because she can't find Bearby."

"Wow. National emergency."

"Yeah. So I'd better go help her. We still on for Tuesday?"

"Absolutely."

Nolan reentered with cups. The aroma reached her before he did. Java! He set them on the creaky table then stuffed Mandy's hospital-acquired things in her Patient Belonging Bag.

"Great. Talk to you then." Mandy hung up after Amelia did.

"Discharge papers?" someone called from the hall.

"In here." Nolan retrieved the forms and tucked them in her lap. And her purse.

"Where did that come from?"

His brows rose. "Stallings?" So did his voice.

Her skin flushed. "Oh. Right. Thanks for thinking about it." Did he remember the childish way she'd tried to test for jealous waters? Hopefully not. She'd never been one for head games, not even in junior high. Maybe her brain collapsed alongside the bridge or something. There had to be a logical explanation for her suddenly neurotic behavior.

Face thoughtful, Nolan laughed spontaneously. "I remember how you used to obsess about forgetting your purse somewhere."

"Even though it never had any money in it." She laughed, too. And it felt good to share that with him again. Better than anything had in a long, long while.

"Which purse?" His face lit with teasing humor. "You changed every week."

His delicious grin carved the stone out of her heart and softened it. She never would have dreamed he would have grown up to be so gorgeous and pack the strength and physique of a first-class hero.

Worthless.

That's what her mother used to call Nolan. Along with her pastor, who agreed he would grow up to amount to nothing.

One look in Nolan's eyes right now, watching him professionally on the bridge yesterday, and hearing him talk of faith told her they'd been dead wrong about him.

Maudlin sentimentality washed over her. She tried to clear her throat and head. "How is my car? Did they say?"

"Not totaled. But close." A grim line stretched across his mouth. "I saw it. I'm surprised and thankful you weren't hurt worse. God protected you, Mandy."

There it was again. A mention of God. As though he knew

Him. Talking about God had never come easy to Nolan. In fact, he used to avoid the subject altogether and certainly never would have initiated a conversation about God.

Could he be a believer now?

If so, how ironic. A twist of the deepest sorrow she'd ever known ground its way up through her. Like a flower reaching through uncultivated earth for the surface of faraway sun.

For the first time in a decade she suddenly felt how far away she was from God. Worlds apart. Kicker was, she hadn't felt anything, God or otherwise, for quite some time.

Nolan wheeled her to the E.R. exit and parked her in the foyer near the waiting room. "Be right back. Let me get my truck."

An absurd sense of panic seized her when he disappeared out the door. She forced her breathing and pounding heart to slow to normal. What was up with that? Her hands trembled, too.

Nolan would come back. He would. Her heart whispered it above the fear that tried to take hold and shake her in a violent grip. She willed her mind to ease the palpitations and streaks of pain shooting through her arm, neck and chest. *This is just the medication, keeping me on edge.*

Nolan's not like Dad.

He'll come back.

But he left once. Abandoned—

No. He's Nolan. He'll do what he says.

But he didn't—

Unforeseen panic welled from nowhere. She suddenly felt like she couldn't get enough air no matter how deep she breathed. Her lips numbed. Her mind flashed back to the bus station. Then the bridge. And suddenly she was there again. Tilting. Screeching tires. Collision. Concrete giving way. Steel bending. Cars in front of her sliding into murky water one after another after another…stopping at hers.

Only it wasn't her car. It was the slam of her dad walking out the door and never coming back. Then it was the bus

Nolan rode away on. His hand on the window. Face in the glass. The urge to run after him yet knowing she couldn't. Then living day after day without him, the atrocious weight of missing him closing in. Hard. Harsh. Unforgiving. Unrelenting. Closing in. Like an angry murderous mob. Surrounding, clawing her. Crushing. Crushing. Crushing her. Even through the sturdy barrier of knowing their parting was as pure and right as was their love yet the timing so wrong. Then weeks. Calling his name.

Nolan.

His name forever on her heart as much as on her lips in prayer as her mind and heart begged for the reprieve of sleep.

Then he came to the bridge. Her feet took her toward him. But he backed up, slipped into the water…yet she was the one left to drown in the dark of its missing—

"Nolan!"

Heaving air, Mandy clutched the arm of the wheelchair and pressed her feet to stand. "But he promised to call. And—and he didn't."

Had she said that aloud? Hand to tightened chest, she fought the urge to yell for oxygen and looked around.

A wide-eyed couple standing in the glass-encased foyer looked at her strangely. The man cast Mandy a sympathetic expression but the woman took a bold step back.

Mandy lowered herself into the seat. Asked herself the same question emanating from their eyes.

God, what's happening to me?

She hadn't lost control like this since she was a teen. Since her best girlfriend's mother walked infidelity like a rabid dog into their home and her father walked out and Mother blamed Mandy for bringing them in. Mandy had learned to cope on her own, since haven could not be found in her home.

Nolan had been her best friend. Talked her through it. No doubt God had used him to get her through it. But she'd grown to depend on him way too much, which had made the pain of his parting way too much.

Now he was back again. Why?

As though cued, a snazzy cobalt blue truck with shiny silver rims and a dashing driver with a dimpled grin pulled up to the Patient Pickup curb.

There he was. He'd come back.

Mandy's mind spun.

She knew what she needed to do.

"Nolan, I—I think I need that anxiety med Riviera offered."

"Panic attack?" Concern filtrated through his attentive expression.

"Yes. Bad. I—I think I might need oxygen. Or something." She loosened her collar and fought to draw in air but there didn't seem to be enough. Pulsing pounded her ears and pressure sat heavier and heavier on her chest. Panic and fear mounted.

She closed her eyes and pressed her hand against her mouth to block the nausea. But images of cars beneath murky liquid under the crumbled bridge gushed like a geyser in her mind.

"Oh, they're drowning! Someone—we have to help them!"

Mandy? A hand on her shoulder. Squeezing. Harder. A shake. *Mandy?* Another shake. Harder.

Mandy, what's wrong?

"Too many—can't get them all—" She tried to run but something held her legs. Cars disappeared until only the eerie brake lights glowed beneath the water. She clawed at the seatbelt harnessing her.

Only not the car. A wheelchair. Where was she?

"Mandy!"

Gasping, she clutched his arm. "Nolan, I'm going to be sick."

One look at her and Nolan flipped the wheelchair brakes off and whirled her around, calling for help. Before Mandy knew it, she was back in a room, a plastic basin beneath her chin. Pulse ox cable nibbled her finger and a needle stung her arm. Bailey dabbed her arm after administering anti-anxiety medication.

"You're fine. Your skin is pink. You are getting enough air," Dr. Riviera said, nose to nose with her. "You're having a panic attack is all."

Her chest squeezed. What if they were wrong? This couldn't just be panic. "No—no—no. I feel like I'm having an MI."

"You're not having a heart attack, Mandy. You had a flashback. Your brain doesn't realize your body is fine. Panic attacks are expected after what you've been through. This is normal. For now."

She looked to Nolan apologetically. Then rage rushed from nowhere. She hadn't wanted him to see her vulnerable. Ever again. And God knew it. And now, He was using this to mock her for ignoring Him all this time. No, that had to be a lie. God wasn't fickle and vengeful like people.

Still, she would not let herself depend on Nolan again. Though sharp interest swam in his leisurely eyes, remembrance of the pain flailed in her heart and mind. No. Mandy made a commitment to her career and settled herself in Refuge with the intent that it be for life. Valiant, internationally needed men like Nolan, world class rescuer and hunk, didn't strap themselves to small towns nor singlehood for long.

She still loved him.

She didn't want to.

She couldn't breathe. Breathing hurt as did seeing him again.

Did she even want to? Or should she try to avoid Nolan at all costs?

If they got back together would he end up walking out like her dad? Pain streaked across Mandy's chest again. Pain trying to take her back to hard places her mind didn't want to go.

Nolan must have seen the shift in her face. He knelt, putting himself inches from her face. "Mandy? What's going on?" he whispered.

She ground her teeth. "I don't want to talk about it."

"Worst thing you can do is hold it in." Blue eyes beckoned her in. Exquisite.

She looked away. "Can you please go get me something to drink?" Anything to get him away so she could regroup. She didn't need to fall apart like this in front of her supervisor. Nor remind Nolan of the weak woman she used to be.

He helped her to the car and she recited her address.

"Come on, Manda-Panda. Let's get you inside."

Mind dazed with meds and heart touched by the verbal endearment, she forced her leaden feet to move.

"Keys?" he asked on her apartment landing.

Still slightly groggy, she dug in her purse several frustrated minutes until he reached out his hand. And grinned. "Some things never change."

Their gazes locked.

No matter how small or organized her purses had been growing up, she always managed to lose her keys inside them. She could even dump her entire purse out, be certain the keys were not in the pile, and look everywhere else.

Then Nolan would reach in her purse without looking, and there'd be her keys. So much so she began calling her purse a quicksand with a leather handle.

"Did you play tricks on me with the keys back then?"

He choked out a laugh but looked very guilty. "No. Women's purses terrify me." That said he reached right in, without looking, and plucked out her key ring.

And grinned like a rake.

She groaned at the injustice while he unlocked the door. Once inside, she sank to her couch.

He crossed her living room casually as if he belonged there, and adjusted her blinds. Then went to the kitchen carrying the plastic-lidded Refuge Memorial pitcher she'd acquired.

Nolan filled it with ice water. "Not your average souvenir. But it'll be handy for nighttime thirst quenching."

She snuggled deep into her worn cushions. "Comfy."

"You should probably go to your bed."

"I'd rather sleep on the couch."

"You always did." He smiled and handed her a fresh cup of coffee.

She vehemently ignored the homesick familiarity creeping up on her. Because along with that surfaced the pain of her dad leaving.

Except she had to know one thing. She peeled back the lid on the coffee he'd brought her. Yup. Nearly white it was so creamy. She sipped. "Some things never change." She thought of the high school bliss of dating Nolan.

"But unfortunately, most things do." The coffee turned sour on her tongue. She set it, and thoughts of Nolan away.

"Not only do I remember how you like your coffee, I still fix it better than you do." He issued a gentle smirk.

Peeling off her shoe, she tossed it at his knee. He swerved his leg and chuckled.

Again, the coffee—like distant memories—called to her. And she had to agree. But she just didn't have to admit so.

Hand curled around the warm cup, she moved the stir stick. Cream swirled like her thoughts. Emotionally, she'd been fine until Nolan showed up on the bridge. Steam wafted from the coffee…just like the cars crushed by concrete entombing cars and people.

Hands trembling, she jammed the lid back on the cup…

And set it aside, with no intention of drinking it. She didn't want anything reminding her of a time she'd loved Nolan. After all, he'd ended up abandoning her, just like her father had.

Chapter Seven

"Thanks for doing this," Nolan said to Miss Ivy, Mandy's landlady and emergency contact who'd agreed to come sit with her. He'd hang for a bit, then go home.

Miss Ivy entered with a satchel of knitting supplies. "I'm glad to. I was a nurse in my younger days. Mandy's been here just shy of a month but I've lost count of how many times she's helped me. Can't drive nowadays so she's my go-to girl." The grandmotherly Miss Ivy smiled toward the couch where a deep sleep consumed Mandy.

Miss Ivy's large St. Bernard squished his nose against her calf and followed her across Mandy's carpet. When Miss Ivy came to rest in the chair the dog plopped down on her feet.

"That dog reminds me of one I used to have. Mandy offered to take care of him when I went off to Air Force boot camp."

"I 'spect by that fond look in your eyes you were a smidgen sweet on her."

Nolan's face flushed. "Maybe a little." Or quite a lot. He hadn't known until he'd left how hard leaving her would be. How much he'd miss her. How much he'd really loved her. Nolan brought two chairs in from the kitchen table and stationed them across from Mandy, whose sparse possessions shocked him. She didn't even own a coffee table.

But she still owns your heart.

Miss Ivy made two cups of instant coffee with supplies in her satchel, then brought a cup to Nolan. As she sat, Nolan felt the weight of eyes having known a lifetime of wisdom resting on his profile.

Nolan took the seat beside Miss Ivy. Resting his cup between his palms, Nolan eyed Mandy. "Growing up, Mandy always loved company."

"I can imagine that. Were you very close?"

Feeling the coffee turn to stone in his throat, Nolan swallowed again but pebbles straddled his tonsils. "Yeah. Real close." He cleared his throat and sipped the brew but the silky liquid still felt like grit. "She never knew what a haven her friendship was to me. Her house was the neighborhood hangout."

Mandy shifted. "Tha'z 'cause Mom wanted to monitor my friends'n my ev'ry move." She turned over.

Nolan resisted the urge to brush wisps of hair from her eyes. "Did we wake you?"

"No, the neighbor's snow blower woke me."

Miss Ivy gave a delicate laugh. Mandy tried to blink awake.

Nolan pulled the cover over her and fended off snickers. "Hate to tell you this, but that snow blower was your nose."

A sleep-bewildered giggle slipped out of Mandy and zinged like a sniper bullet straight to Nolan's unsuspecting heart. He should have seen this coming.

He'd never stopped loving her.

The thought lodged in his throat. He reached for her DVD basket.

Mandy maneuvered to sitting. "What are we watching?"

"*We* are watching a movie. *You* are going back to sleep." He fluffed her pillow. She blinked slowly and had that lights-on-but-nobody's-home look. Eyelids drooped. Torso wavered, then see-sawed sideways, sideways, down. Nolan steered so she didn't hang off the couch.

Miss Ivy chuckled. "Asleep before her head even hit the pillow.

"Is she having a hard time coping?" Miss Ivy asked in low tones.

"As one would expect." In addition, she'd exhibited signs of Post Traumatic Stress Disorder, which concerned him greatly.

Mandy shifted. Her hand collided with the lamp. She whimpered.

Nodding toward the bedroom, Nolan rose. "Miss Ivy, could you turn down her covers?"

"Moving her to her room?"

"Yeah. She'll sleep better and be less likely to hurt herself." Nolan slid careful hands beneath Mandy's waist and knees and scooped her up. She started to blink awake. When her eyes lit on Nolan, she relaxed.

He set her down on the bottom sheet and pulled the covers up to her chin. Then barricaded her arm with pillows. Miss Ivy came in with the water pitcher.

"Thanks."

Miss Ivy retreated.

Nolan went to click off Mandy's bedside light. He started to step away but Mandy's face beckoned him back. Gone were the tense lines that had given away her barely contained hostility before. Hostility that clued him in that she still had remnants of bitterness. Which meant they still had issues to resolve between them. Now, sleep and moonlight bathed her face in peace.

This is the part of you I remember.

His left hand came up to press into the place between his chest and throat. But the burn went too deep to rub away. Before his mind reconciled why, his other hand stretched to brush tendrils of hair off her forehead. Fingertips only.

Just a minute more of admiring, and he'd go. He let his eyes drink deeply of a face magnificent to behold. One he'd seen change through their neighborhood years together. From the soft innocence of childhood, through the acne of puberty, the womanly air that her face had finally grown into.

Doubt and thoughts assaulted him. What if he'd tried harder to reach her back then? What if they'd made a way to stay together? Would she still have managed to get this far with medical school?

Knowing Mandy then, no.

But today's Mandy suggested she possessed a strength, a drive, a perseverance and an independence like never before.

Maybe because it hadn't been there before?

Maybe it had taken her seeing she could survive without him and do this on her own in order for her to run after her dream?

He didn't know. But he did know this: He'd made the right choice in breaking things off ten years ago. Had to believe it. Much as his heart ached to know what the last ten years of her life had been like. Despite the ache that taunted him with the knowledge that he hadn't gotten to share it or watch her grow into the person she was.

"Nolan?" Mandy started to sit up.

"Shh. Go back to sleep."

"Is someone here with you?" She blinked but the grog didn't detach from her eyes.

"I didn't feel comfortable leaving you alone. Miss Ivy will stay with you tonight."

As though hearing her name, Miss Ivy entered. "How is she?"

"Restless."

Nolan clicked off Mandy's light, then made a pharmacy run and returned with Mandy's prescriptions. Mandy's recliner cradled Miss Ivy as she contentedly knitted. Nolan dug the bottle of pain reliever from the bag and ignored the money beside it.

"She'll have a conniption when she finds out you didn't use her money to pay." Miss Ivy's mouth twitched as she knitted.

"Probably so." He smiled knowing she was right and feeling good that Mandy had a mother figure close by. Mandy and her mother had grown apart after Mandy's dad abandoned the two. Mandy'd looked to Nolan to meet all of her emotional needs. But he'd seen strengths that she might never have discovered in herself had he not made the decision to enlist.

Nolan helped Miss Ivy wash the dishes in Mandy's sink, then prepared to leave. He set the TV remote near Mandy and turned it on to a worship station, remembering she liked sleeping with music. Unable to find a Bible anywhere in the house, he removed his from the rucksack. Miss Ivy eyed him curiously.

"I need her to know what a difference she made in my life." Mandy hadn't commented when he'd brought up God.

"I can't bear the thought that the person most responsible for planting those early seeds that have now grown into faith has fled the garden and never looked back."

Nolan flicked on the nightlight and set his Bible next to her on the table so she wouldn't have to stumble around in darkness.

He scribbled his number down in case she needed a ride anywhere later. She wouldn't be able to drive for weeks. He left the forms the doctor had given her beneath the Bible.

Room temperature adjusted, he knelt beside her. For the longest moments, he watched her sleep. Felt weird staring with her unaware, so he forced himself to stop.

He placed a gentle hand on her forehead. *Keep her safe. Help her heal quickly. And most of all bring her back where she belongs…close to You.*

Nolan rose, fighting the urge to bed down on her couch. What if she developed a blood clot or a life-threatening wound infection overnight? Would Miss Ivy know what to do?

What if he stopped staring and fearing the worst and trusted God to watch out for Mandy instead?

Plus his space on the team was now an endangered species.

Tomorrow could be one of the most difficult days of his life. Petrowski, and Joel by teleconference, were meeting with military officials at Refuge Air Base to launch a series of meetings which could make or break Nolan's place on the team. He needed to be there. Couldn't abandon his brothers or his creed. Not even for Mandy.

It is my duty as a pararescueman to save life and to aid the injured. I will perform my assigned duties quickly and efficiently, placing these duties before personal desires and comforts. These things I do, "That Others May Live."

If the meeting didn't go favorably, tomorrow would be the beginning of the end of life as he knew it. It could also mean the possible loss of all the things he held dear. A sacrifice he'd make for his creed and his country. Not just the brotherhood and closeness of his team and their families.

But also the newfound dreams of reconciling his relationship with Mandy.

Chapter Eight

The evidence was everywhere. Nolan had stayed a while.

And obviously he'd intended her to know it. Her dishes were washed and drying in the drain. A camouflage-detailed Bible lay open in the book of Psalms beside her. Psalms had been her favorite book. Gold calligraphic letters scrolled across the lower right corner of the Bible's cover. Letters bearing Nolan's name, proving what she'd suspected: his name also now rested in God's Book of Life.

How she had prayed for that growing up. Yet it had never happened. And how she'd prayed for God to make a way for them to be together…something else that never happened. Just like when her parents never got back together and her dad never chose to return to his family. The rejections stung worse than words could describe.

Rage simmered like water in the kettle on her stove. She let out a sound not unlike the whistle blown by pent-up pressure. She didn't know which irked her more—the idea he was sending her a message or the fact that he was trying to waltz back into her life like the past had never happened.

Bored and irritated, Mandy stepped into the hall that led to the outer door for her newspaper and fresh air.

Miss Ivy, who also lived in the two-hundred year-old home, passed by on her way to walk her dog. "Your young man just left a couple of hours ago."

Mandy flushed. "We're just friends." It surprised Mandy how much it stung to say those words. She rubbed her arm. Mandy walked Miss Ivy to the door to let the dog do his business.

The landlady's cheeks shifted upward as she smiled. "Nice man, that Nolan."

"Hmm." Mandy followed, assisting Miss Ivy down the step.

"He was kind enough to have a cup of coffee with me before he left." Miss Ivy studied Mandy.

"Oh." What else could she say? And why was the spry Miss Ivy studying her like a cardiologist with a bad EKG?

"I'm glad you have friends who care enough about you to keep you company while you recover from such a horrible ordeal." She stretched up and cupped Mandy's cheek, then planted a grandmotherly kiss there. "And I'm glad you ended up all right."

Robotic, Mandy nodded, feeling far from all right. She didn't want to take any more anti-anxiety or pain meds because they just plain knocked her out.

Being around Miss Ivy always made her miss her mother. Today was no exception.

Mandy's mom had left frantic messages since the collapse. Though she and Mom didn't exactly get along these days, Mandy had tried to call to let her know what had happened rather than have her see images on national TV.

Having knelt to pet the dog, Mandy rose and smiled at Miss Ivy. "I'd better let you walk him. He might drag you off otherwise." Mandy reached down and scrubbed the St. Bernard behind his ears.

As Miss Ivy and the dog stepped out into the sunshine, an image of the similar dog Mandy had growing up bounded into her mind.

Mandy decided to join Miss Ivy in her walk. "He looks so much like Nolan's old dog." She swallowed but the emotion wouldn't budge. Nor would the memories of good times with Nolan and the want for them again.

"Is that so?" Miss Ivy adjusted the leash.

"After Nolan, that St. Bernard was my best friend."

Soon, they finished walking the dog. Miss Ivy remained outside near her flower garden and Mandy reentered Ivy Manor.

Feeling old sorrow sweep through her, Mandy picked up the newspaper from the inner walkway. Looked at the words but comprehension eluded her. She rubbed her arm. That icky feeling still crept over her skin. Grating across every nerve ending. Turned her arms into twitching extensions of how her insides felt.

"Argh!" The urge to run through the hallway screaming accosted Mandy. What was the deal? Where was her even keel? And why all these emotional outbursts? Undoubtedly the double whammies of the bridge collapse and Nolan's return triggered the traumatic memories of her dad leaving in her teens. Distraction would help. She'd feel better in sunlight.

"This hallway is too dark." Exiting, Mandy prepared to walk around the property and enjoy Miss Ivy's burgundy knockout roses and crepe myrtle plants. Charcoal and grilled meat aromas enticed the air. Moisture erupted in her mouth. Though she wondered who in their right minds grilled meat for breakfast. She eyed her watch. Never mind. It was noon.

What was wrong with her that she couldn't keep track of time since the collapse? Like she tumbled in a trance-state all the time. In this realm peace did not exist.

Maybe she could take up jogging. Expend this pent-up energy making her feel like screaming until she expelled her lungs and this thing clinging to her diaphragm that made breathing hard.

Halfway around the house, wet splats landed on Mandy's

arm. She looked up. Raindrops tinkled over her face. "So much for jogging."

"You jog?" Miss Ivy turned to head back, too.

"No. Thought about taking it up. Then came to my senses."

That made Miss Ivy laugh as they scurried for shelter.

Mandy held the newspaper over Miss Ivy's snowy head while they rushed inside. The dog's tags jingled as they ran.

"At least I don't have to water my flowers today. So maybe we can invite your Nolan over for sandwiches instead."

Your Nolan? "Or not."

The women shared a laugh.

"Miss Ivy, I love that friendship is strong enough to span generations."

"And I love that I haven't had to water my outside plants or pull my weeds once since you moved here."

Mandy laughed. Glad too since it helped ease the anxiety pulsing through her nerves in waves.

Miss Ivy's dog jerked her down the hall. "See you later, Mandy."

They entered their respective apartments. Mandy tossed the soggy newspaper in the waste can.

Black ink mussed her hands. She washed them, then put on a fresh cup of Caramel Colada Coffee, one of several homespun specialty coffees from Square Beans, a local coffeehouse on the town square in Refuge. A square that was actually round. Another strange yet endearing quality of the quaint and quirky town known to live up to its name.

Then this horrible bridge collapse. And she was there again. Black memories submerged her like cars. Screaming. People. Dark water. Deep. Death. No way to help. Help. Too many. No time. A far from civilized cry ripped from her throat, shredding her control. Her legs trembled. Hands quavered. Nausea struck. Dizziness. Memories. Blue water turned black. She needed to sit. Now.

Face in hands, Mandy panted. "Calm down." Deep breaths would help. Should help. They didn't.

A door slammed down the hall. Her body jerked in response. Reminded her of Dad leaving. And steel bending. And Nolan.

Could Refuge still feel like a haven? Even with Nolan here? Yes. Healing would come. Refuge was.

Or maybe it was because he was here. Mandy picked up her purse and fumbled for her anti-anxiety medication.

A half hour later calm came. But drugs were only a Band-Aid. And they weren't effective for soul scrapes and spirit wounds.

"I know what I have to do." And she knew to Whom she spoke. She had to hash things out with Nolan and recover her relationship with God. Revive her faith in Jesus and His love.

Once seated with the sweet, steaming coffee, Mandy pulled Nolan's camouflage Bible close and looked through it. Amazing the notes he'd written in it.

The front inscription said it had been given to him by someone named Joel. She wondered who he was. Someone on Nolan's PJ team no doubt, since she'd heard Nolan mention the name yesterday. Or maybe she'd heard his name on the bridge. Mandy set the Bible aside.

Bridge.

At the very thought, images surged in and filled her mind like water filled the cars. Cars with people in them. Sordid images and hellacious sounds took her mind hostage. "No!" Stop. How could she stop it? Her hands trembled.

More images. This time of cars crushed on the bridge as she ran past, trying to find someone. Someone not too far gone to help. Then the children crying. Then seeing them on the bus and not knowing the best thing to do.

Then seeing the body bag on the gurney. Finding out the truck driver she'd bypassed to help them died on the bridge as he crawled as far as he could for help.

Stress from that sent pain streaking up both sides of her neck.

She tried and tried to close her mind. Fought to block out images. Fought and lost. Why wasn't the medicine working?

I know I've been far from You. And I far from deserve it. But I'm drowning in trauma. Please help me.

Her phone rang. She snatched it from her purse and viewed caller ID. Amelia. Relief flooded her. Calm came within her grasp. The knowledge that He'd answered so fast sank steadying anchors for her as if she was a boat tossed in an unruly storm.

Thank you.

"Hey."

"Hey." Amelia sounded momentarily startled. "I had the strongest urge to call. Are you okay?"

"You really want to know?"

"Yes."

"I'm terrible." Mandy sank back into the couch and rubbed her temple with the edge of her cast. "I'm not sure. I'm feeling a headache coming on. Having horrible flashbacks, too, I think."

"Let me pray for you, Mandy."

So Amelia was a Christian, too. She proceeded to pray right then and there on the phone.

Another achy void burrowed beneath her ribs, unleashing a powerful longing she didn't know she had to be firmly "in" with God again.

"Thank you. The images did lift some." Not a lie. Her trembling got marginally better, too. But her head still pounded and possessed that space helmet feeling she got right before a migraine. "Have you ever had long hair and cut it?" Mandy asked.

Amelia grew silent. "Uh, yes. Why?"

"Just wondered if, after you cut it short, did you feel the compulsion to go around telling every gorgeously long-haired girl or cute guy that you used to have long hair, too?"

Amelia giggled. "I did, actually. But I thought I was the only weirdo."

Mandy laughed, too. "Well, my severed faith is that way. I used to pray. A long time ago. And be close to God." Emotion burned behind her eyes. "I'm not even sure why I feel the need to tell you that. Other than I guess I just miss Him. And I thought you'd want to know that I—I used to know Him, too."

An empathetic sound came through the phone. "Mandy, I know at least one thing we have in common then. I didn't walk with God for a season. It's when Reece was conceived. God will take you back in a heartbeat. You know that, right?"

"I just don't know if we can ever be that close. It's been nearly ten years. And I'm ashamed that I've ignored Him for so long. And I hurt at the thought of the closeness I've missed. The lack of obedience. Doesn't seem fair, to Him I mean, or to others who never strayed that He'd bring me right back into that kind of closeness."

Mandy's own words boomeranged regarding Nolan.

…trying to waltz back into her life like the chasm never happened.

"Don't let those lies keep you away from Him. We might walk away and we may even forget. But He loves us even in times when we take no thought of Him," Amelia said.

"Thank you," Mandy choked past rawness that refused to remain bottled.

"Are the images you're having of the collapse?"

Relief fluttered through Mandy that Amelia had the sensitivity to know when to change the subject.

God, we might not be on great speaking terms yet, but I know what You did for me and those children on the bridge. And I refuse to live life without thanking You. I'm grateful for this new friend. And that You sent her.

The prayer wrought peace. A sense of joy and relief that her heart was leaning, reaching, yearning toward Jesus again.

Thank you for that, too. I know it comes from You.

Amelia didn't seem fazed by her silence. The sign of a true friend. Not feeling the need to fill empty emotional space with surface-level words. Sometimes silence spoke deep things between friends when words would ruin the moment.

After a shuddering sigh, Mandy pulled in the longest, most refreshing breath of her life.

"Yes. Images of the collapse." And the shock of seeing Nolan again. She didn't know which had been more traumatic. Should she mention it to Amelia yet? Obviously Nolan…what was she about to think? Oh, well.

"Mandy?"

"Sorry. My train of thought derailed again. That's been happening almost constantly since the collapse. Difficulty concentrating and all sorts of emotional outbursts. Physical symptoms, too. Stomachaches. No appetite. And believe me, when I'm not eating, something is very, very wrong."

The women shared a laugh, but Amelia's faded into a seriousness that felt tangible across the line. "Are you sleeping okay now?"

"No. That's part of it, I think. Even when I finally manage to fall asleep it's restless and I have nightmares of the collapse." And of Dad and of falling for Nolan and them leaving again.

Knocks sounded on the door. "Listen, someone's here. I'll call you back." After Amelia replied, Mandy hung up and headed for the door.

"Afternoon." The point of her heart's contention stood there. Nolan, looking cuter than a man had right to. A bag of what smelled like a mouthwatering lunch in hand. "Thought you might be hungry. You're supposed to take your meds with food and I doubted you'd feel like cooking." Dimples that deep should be illegal. They disrupted the workings of her heart. A heart longing to be close again.

She stepped aside to let him in.

He eyed the open Bible and grinned widely. "You found it."

"Yeah. Big surprise." She shuffled foot to foot and licked her lips, hating that she had read his personal information in the front and his study notes and his prayer requests in the margins. Embarrassment raked against her that she might have violated his privacy. But, he knew her curious nature and after all, he had left the Bible here on purpose.

Still, why hadn't he tried to have a relationship with God while the two of them were young? Maybe then, they would have had a chance. Anger stormed through her, as did the urge to lash out like a hurt animal. "I never figured you for a holy roller."

His grin vanished. Instant remorse hit her. Everything in her wanted to reach for him but instead she felt frozen.

He strode inside, fluid and panther-fast. "If you're saying those things to shock me, it's not going to work. I know you know the truth. Don't pretend you don't." Things clunked when he set the bag on the counter a little hard.

Nolan's tense movements and stubbornly jutted jaw caused her to take pause. Hand braced on the counter, she held very still, unaccustomed to seeing Nolan be so passionate about issues of faith. And completely unprepared for how it caused her heart to tumble with longing.

A ten-year-old cynical lump began dissolving as she observed him. "I—I don't know what I believe anymore," she blurted. Then scowled at herself for being a sliver of real.

"Wow. Grumpy today."

"I'm sorry. What I said was uncalled for. It doesn't help that I have a headache."

"You're going through a lot." The object of her silent wrath and secret awe handed her a burrito. Something melted in her that he remembered how well she liked them, and surprised her when he also pulled one out for himself.

"You never liked those." She positioned herself so he could pass but instead he stood inches away. He had the audacity to grin.

She evaded him, heading toward the kitchen but he moved in her path again. He lifted a hand and grazed the side of her cheek with his knuckles. It took every cell of strength not to lean into his touch.

Humor sparkled in his gentle eyes. "There are a lot of ways I've changed that you don't know about yet." His gaze dropped to her mouth.

Yet?

Speaking of mouth, hers went dry at his look of bold determination.

Then like a dimmer switch, his hand and eyes disengaged. He headed for the door.

Was he leaving? She stepped toward him but he merely pushed the door closed with his foot.

"What, like you suddenly found God?" She hid her grin and followed him into the kitchen. How she missed their verbal sparring. Maybe it wouldn't hurt to poke a little. Just a little. "Well?"

"Didn't find Him. He found me after pursuing me a lifetime with love more relentless and powerful than anything I've ever known." His expression turned deeply grateful and deadpan serious. Something daring in his tone demanded that she remember that God could recapture her heart, too.

Something in her threatened to crack. She rubbed her arm and turned away. Before an impending emotional outburst could give her away. If she broke, she didn't want Nolan to see.

"You were restless last night." He took clean plates out of her dish drainer.

"Slept better than I have been, though."

"Nightmares?"

She nodded.

"Bad ones?"

"Yes. About the bridge collapse."

"Might want to consider seeing a counselor."

She shrugged. "I'm sure it'll pass. Thanks for doing my dishes, by the way."

"You're welcome. Actually, Miss Ivy helped."

"But she said it was your idea."

Hazy memories of Nolan filling her water pitcher and helping her take her meds flashed back. In one of Mandy's more coherent moments, he'd talked and Mandy listened. Something about his superiors wanting to pluck him from the team.

She'd regretted asking about his job. If she fell back in love with him, the threat of his leaving could cause a trail of devastation in her carefully ordered life.

"Seriously, Nolan, thank you for staying and arranging for Miss Ivy to help. I appreciated the company. My nightmares would have been worse had I been here alone."

"You don't ever have to be alone again, Mandy." Pausing in his task of putting their burritos on plates, Nolan peered at her over his shoulder, stapling her feet to the floor. "And the nightmares don't have to be yours if you'll let me in to help you. They could be ours to conquer together." His voice had dropped to raw octaves of all kinds of deep emotion, and possibilities of an uncertain future that she didn't want to explore.

Though their love could be steel-beam-strong, their careers were too crumbling-concrete-uncertain and their prior commitments incompatible. No way could she leap off this kind of bridge again. Because love was like Reunion Bridge over Refuge. Not secure. Things could fall through without warning. And the results could be catastrophic to her emotions and heart.

And she couldn't cross that path again.

* * *

Nolan pulled a chair out and motioned for her to sit. He cringed. Hopefully he hadn't scratched the floor. Not that it would matter, as scuffed as the tiles were.

"Later, I'll take a gander at that. Figure out why your chair's so lopsided. Fix it for you."

Her gaze averted. "That's not necessary."

Great. Now he'd gone and embarrassed her. Platitude stifled, he slid a plate toward her, then joined her across the table.

She reached for her fork but he reached for her.

Pink tinged her cheeks. She lowered the utensil and stared at him with eyes that widened by the second.

"Let's say grace." He squeezed her hand and lowered his head.

Afterward, he took a bite of the burrito. He'd started eating them because they reminded him of her. They'd grown on him for that reason alone. It was a connection to her. He wondered how she'd react or what she'd think if he told her that.

Chewing, he nodded toward her plate where her fork jabbed food around in aimless circles. "You should try a few bites at least."

"Funny. I don't much care for them anymore." She leaned back and her face transformed into a challenge that dared him to think the burritos were anything but detestable. The harshness in her tone took him aback. Like she would violently resist anything that reminded her of him or their past time together.

Except for the panda necklace. His eyes shot to her neck. No necklace.

"It's gone."

Her hand went where his gaze remained. "I took it off."

She didn't have to tell him the rest. She took it off…for the first time since the day he'd given it to her fourteen years ago.

A heavy sadness settled over him. He set his burrito down, too, suddenly losing his own appetite.

The missing necklace sent him a message.

She didn't need it anymore. Or him. Furthermore she didn't want to be reminded of the years she had.

But who was she trying to convince?

He knew her rage and emotional outbursts were probably a result of PTSD. So he wouldn't take it personally.

Nolan reached across the table for her hand. Surprisingly, she let him.

Her purse suddenly chimed. She started to rise but he reached behind him. Tugged her purse off the counter and set it in front of her. Mandy rifled through it.

He snickered.

She shot a rueful smile at him.

The phone continued to chime.

She continued to claw her way to the bottom of the Grand Canyon aka her purse.

Elbow on the table, he pressed his finger over his mouth. "Wild Thing" continued to chime. Setting it in her lap, she blew a breath out which fluttered the bangs off her forehead. She dug through her purse like a madwoman.

"Do you want me to—?"

"No."

"After all, you're short a hand and it'd be faster if I—"

"I'm fine." More frantic shuffling through the purse. The song stopped and a series of bleeps sounded. Her eyes rolled.

Hard as it was, he resisted the urge to ignore her protest and help. Maybe he should have because by the time she got to it, the call had gone to voice mail. Mandy groaned.

She eyed the phone screen. "I forgot to call this person back. Excuse me." She rose.

Gathering their trash, he stood, too. "That's okay. I need to get going anyhow. Have other stuff to do today." Such as another meeting that would begin to decide the fate of his place on the team. Should he tell her?

There was a wall the altitude of Everest erected between them now. Hostility clawing to the surface. He saw it every time he looked in her eyes until she veiled it. Heard it on the jagged edges of incisive words. The thought of how bad it must have hurt her to think he'd abandoned her cut him to the core. Though they'd hashed out that conversation before he'd enlisted and she'd supported his decision and agreed they should break up, and their minds accepted the fact, he hadn't anticipated that her heart would still feel abandoned.

Hadn't Mandy read a single one of the letters he sent?

An unsettling feeling came over him that she hadn't.

Why?

And if so, why hadn't she written back? He'd just assumed she'd moved on. Last night, she'd genuinely wanted to hear about his job, proving she was happy he'd realized his dream. And he'd been honest about his place on the Refuge PJ team being in jeopardy. But he wouldn't further burden her with his struggles. Nor would he mention the letters. Because if the interceptor was who he suspected, the knowledge would only hurt Mandy further.

Sadness and a strange sense of panic hounded him. He'd always confided in her because he knew, without a doubt, he could count on her prayers. And Mandy's prayers packed a punch. So many people had depended on her gift of praying for others.

How he missed her prayers and could really use them right now. All these things that had sounded so foreign to him growing up when she'd mention them had left him intrigued. But not necessarily interested enough to pursue her religion.

Not until he'd joined the pararescue team, met Joel and witnessed Joel's genuine relationship with God did he begin to understand Mandy's growing up. Now, the terms meant everything to him and nothing to her.

Forgive her. Draw her back to who she's meant to be. I

know You miss her prayers. I know how much they impacted my life, though I never wanted to admit it back then.

While she chatted on the phone in the other room, desperation caused him to reach for a notebook in his Bible. He scribbled the words:

 # 157. Remember how you always used to tell me that God never takes a person's gifts away, even if they don't use them for Him? I do. Another thing you always used to tell me is that God's love doesn't waver even when we walk. I hope somewhere inside you still remember that, Manda Panda, and know that He still loves you, even when you don't serve Him. But I know what kind of impact you had in my life. I hope you find your faith again because people need your prayers. Me being one of them. And baby, if God misses you half as much as I do, then all of Heaven cries for you, Mandy. He longs to have you back.

And so do I. He thought but didn't write.

Please reconsider. Love, Nolan.

Nolan folded the paper and stuffed it under the Bible.

As a Christian, a deep sense of grief washed over him for Mandy's lost faith. He'd do anything to help restore it.

After ending her phone conversation, Mandy walked Nolan to the door. "Thank you for bringing lunch. I didn't mean to sound ungrateful. I didn't take into consideration how your work must be piling up with you spending time here."

He grinned. "Nothing's piling up. Early morning, before I get here. I jump. Then at night, too." Practicing HALOs. "Weather's been perfect for it."

"You get paid every time you jump?"

"Yep. Three hundred bucks a parachute pop."

"That's it? Even for HALOs? Those are infinitely more dangerous."

He couldn't stifle a goofy grin or pleasant surprise flitting through him. "You know about HALOs?"

"I'm well versed about pararescue. Seems I recall HALOs are the kind where you jump from altitudes requiring oxygen and you don't open the parachute until you're very close to the ground. Hence the HALO acronym—High-Altitude, Low-Opening."

He braced hands above his head on the door facing. "You studied pararescue?" He could giggle like a kid with glee.

She dipped her head but peered at him through bangs that had fallen over suddenly shy eyes. "I know more about your profession than you'd ever dream, Nolan." Wistfulness in her voice grounded him in the moment.

His mouth went dry and his pulse went crazy. Deep breath. Nolan shifted. "How'd you learn what you know?"

"About?" Slow, an unseen hook tugged her chin skyward. "Pararescue."

She sniffed and something registered in her features that told him she was mentally measuring how much information to reveal.

"Libraries. Books. News articles. The Internet. You name it."

"You went to that much trouble?"

Her shrug didn't convince. And averted eyes didn't hide.

Overcome with emotion for her, he lowered his hand to cup her cheek again. "Mandy?" he whispered with a hoarseness not there a moment ago.

Her face lifted and that haunted look returned to her eyes as they locked in tandem with his. "Yes. I used to study it every five minutes, thinking maybe I'd get a glimpse of you on one of those Air Force military Web sites."

His thumb brushed the slope of her cheekbone.

Hand covering his, she gave a lighthearted shrug and looked at the carpet fibers. "Occasionally I still, you know, check it out online. Lately, not much." She turned her face, forcing him to drop the hand that only ached to hold her.

She rubbed her hand along her arm, or rather, the sling. The familiar motion thrust him back in time.

She always used to rub her arms when anxious. But never in his presence. Except the first time he kissed her in a park when they were teens the day their friendship matured into more.

He'd really love to repeat that kiss scenario. Right here and now would be good. But she'd tuck tail and run.

Dreamy amazement floated over her face like a well-steered parachutist's jump-boots brushing the earth in stable landing. "It's awe-inspiring what you PJs do. I mean, how crazy great is it that astronauts have your team on their speed dial? They know if something goes amiss, you're the first ones they want."

For a moment, when her face tilted up, a flash of the starry-eyed hero worship she always used to stare at him with every time he'd come to her rescue hovered in her eyes.

Now things called for a spiritual rescue. But maybe that was God's gig and not his? *Show me my part in this, if any.*

"It's awe-inspiring that you know as much as you do about pararescue," he said.

Which suggested she'd not been able to put him completely out of her mind through the years. And implications of that suggestion sent his heart and hope skyward.

Despite her current defense mechanism to block whatever God was doing here, there was hope for them.

It was more than he could ask for. Let alone that he'd been asking God night and day to restore her faith and revive her relationship with Him foremost.

A knock sounded. Mandy rose to answer it. Nolan was closer. "I'll get it." He opened the door.

Then wished he hadn't.

Mandy's mom, Marva, stood on the other side.

She gasped. "Well, Nolan Briggs? What are you doing here?" Marva shoved past him and bulldozed across the living room. Nolan clenched his jaw. His bad day just got worse.

Mandy stood, looking at Nolan as if he'd brought her mom here. "Mom! What are you doing here?"

"You were in a bridge collapse! I had to see for myself you were okay." Marva looked Mandy up and down and ignored Nolan.

Great. One more thing to challenge a rebuilding of the friendship, and possible relationship, of him and Mandy.

He turned to study the woman who looked much older than he remembered. Something else unsettled him. She looked pale. A sickly kind of pale. And thin to the point of gauntness.

"Mother, what's wrong with you?"

"What do you mean?" Marva slid out of her jacket. Nolan hung it up for her.

"You've lost weight you didn't need to."

Marva shrugged and headed for the kitchen.

Casting Nolan a concerned expression, Mandy followed, pushing her sleeves up. "Mother, you don't look good. What's wrong?"

Marva turned on the water, effectively drowning out her daughter's voice. Just like old times. Nolan felt like saying it but bit his tongue.

"I'm sick at the thought of you two living together without telling me."

Mandy gasped. "Mother! That's not true. I just met him again on the bridge."

"Right."

Nolan stepped forward. "We haven't seen each other in ten years. Besides that, I've changed."

Marva turned on the garbage disposal, drowning him out, too.

Nolan eyed his watch. He needed to leave now to make his meeting. Besides, Mandy and her mom obviously needed to talk. He headed for the door. Before he said something he'd regret.

"See you later, Mandy."

She whirled, giving him a panicked don't-leave-me-alone-with-her look.

Marva said nothing.

Mandy observed her, then Nolan, and straightened. "Okay, bye."

He studied her face on his way out the door. A face that was trying to be blank yet was full of ambivalence and turmoil. No doubt the outer battle resembled the one in her heart.

I know how much I miss her. Can't imagine how much more You do. Determination gritted his teeth until they hurt.

Joel and Manny, his spiritual mentors, always said to just come right out and tell God what you wanted. Be honest, because He already reads minds and hearts anyway.

And what was the deal with Marva showing up? Of course she would. She was Mandy's mother. He fought bitterness over the control she'd exerted and the spiritual abuse Mandy had endured under the leadership of the pastor her mother so adored.

But Mandy was right. Marva didn't look good. Something was wrong. Physically very wrong with her.

Nolan stepped out onto the landing, but pressed his hand against Mandy's closed door. "If that be the case, beckon her back, Lord. Much as I want to pray 'Not Your will but mine be done,' instead I ask if it be Your will, please help me win her heart back, too. And, hard as it is to ask, help Marva see a doctor."

"Everything all right, Nolan?" Miss Ivy approached with her head cocked back in query.

Nolan pushed away from the door and smiled. "It will be."

The humongous dog on the end of her leash pranced around.

"Hey, buddy." He knelt to scrub her dog behind the ears. "I had a St. Bernard like you growing up." Before he'd given the dog to Mandy and left. He closed his mouth before the knot could form in his throat.

"Where did your families live before?"

"Tennessee."

"What took you apart? Because entangled hearts become oblivious to age. And you both have the look of two young people who have loved and lost and hurt over one another deeply."

He nodded, knowing he couldn't refute any of that. "We do have a rich history. She graduated a year after me. She went to Seattle to med school on a scholarship provided by her church. I joined the Air Force."

"Tennessee. Didn't know she'd lived there. I knew she lived in Seattle because she's always saying she's glad to be rid of the unrelenting rain."

Nolan stepped away from Mandy's door and leaned against the wall. "Really?" He loved hearing about Mandy but didn't want her to feel like he was stalking.

"Yes. I'm sure God brought her to Refuge." Her eyes twinkled. "And maybe He brought you here, too. And maybe the two of you will have a second chance. God is drawing her in many ways, Nolan."

All of Heaven cries for you to come back, Mandy.

Chill bumps broke out all over Nolan's arms and marched across the top of his head and down his spine.

Because truth was, when he'd written that, he hadn't given it forethought, nor had he even known what he meant or even why he was writing that. It was just the impression that came to mind.

Outer door pressed open with her hand, the dog tugged her into sunlight. She beamed at him over slightly hunched shoulders. "Thought I'd mention the breeder I got my dog from let me know she has a litter ready to wean." She tilted her head back to eye Mandy's door. "She won't probably admit this, but I know she gets lonely at night."

An idea formed. "I see what you're getting at. You wouldn't mind your tenants having a dog?"

"No. Especially not her. If those stars in your eyes when you talk about her are an indication of romantic interest, then you still think she's as special as I do."

If he were shy like Chance, he'd blush. So he just grinned instead. "Where's the breeder located?"

As Miss Ivy relayed the information, Nolan committed it to memory. Then as the huge St. Bernard lugged the landlady down her sidewalk, Nolan prayed like crazy Mandy would respond favorably to what he had in mind. The more time he spent around Mandy, the more concerned he grew that she was exhibiting PTSD. The companionship of a dog would be therapeutic.

And maybe, just maybe, if he gifted her with the cutest puppy in the bunch, her soft spot for Nolan would grow, too.

Chapter Nine

"No." Mandy stabbed Nolan with death-threat looks and shoved to her feet from where she sat on the couch at the breeder's home.

"But he's cute."

"So are you, but I'm not giving in to either of you." Arms folded, she stepped away from the dog. Far away. He eyed her with a sappy, expectant expression.

So did Nolan. He gestured to the dog. "Look. Mooch is panting his pleasure at your mere presence." He gave royal arm waves.

"Mooch? You already named the dog?" Her good hand zipped to her hip. Suspicion glazed her eyes.

Nolan straightened. "Hey, wait. You still think I'm cute?"

She did the eye-roll thing.

"That's what you said."

Pink powdered her cheeks. "So I did. But at the moment, you're not as cute as Mooch. Although if I were him, I'd bite your fingers off for putting that ridiculous white and black polka dot *thing* on his head," Mandy said as she plucked at the ribbon.

"It's a pretty bow."

"Macho boy dogs don't wear polka dot bows any more than PJs stray from clear blue skies."

Nolan laughed.

Annoyed lines pulled her eyebrows together. "Poor baby pooch. How insulted you must feel to have this girlie gizmo on."

The dog stretched his neck and licked her hand. She jerked it away, wiped it on her jeans then stuffed it under her sling.

Nolan scrubbed the St. Bernard puppy beneath his chin but looked at Mandy. "You love black and silvery-white. The snazzy boy bow is because he is a gift from me to you."

Her chin lowered. "For what?"

"Isn't there a Doctor's Day or something?"

She wilted him with a *get real* look, but a smile teased her mouth.

"Does there have to be a reason?" Nolan glanced where the breeder was visible through the patio glass, feeding the other puppies. And, Nolan suspected, to give them time to talk.

Mandy looked everywhere but the dog. "I don't want him—it."

At her voice, the puppy cocked his head. His mouth panted in a perpetual grin and his body quivered in anticipation.

"Besides, my mom hates dogs."

"How long is she staying?" Nolan asked.

Mandy shrugged. "Until Friday. She has some follow up tests back home."

"For?"

"She won't say. And I don't want to speculate." Her hands trembled. She let out a frustrated sound.

The puppy bumped her forearm with his nose.

Her gaze dropped to the dog. "No."

Mooch yipped and pressed his paw into her shin.

She groaned and eyed Nolan. "Last thing I need right now is a dog I have to clean up after." She raised her elbow. "Especially with broken bones. And my mom possibly being sick."

"I planned to come over and help you." But he was more concerned about Mandy and her mother now. Maybe this had been a mistake. Yet he knew that animals as companions could be therapeutic for PTSD, which he was sure Mandy had.

"Oh, joy. Another reason to refuse the dog." She smirked.

"Ouch." Nolan put his hand to his chest. "For a healer, you sure know how to wound." The smile never left his eyes. "I'll potty-train him and everything. Even take him for walks with you if that'll help make the transition easier."

"No. Absolutely not. No dog. Period."

The puppy lunged forward, leapt and put both paws on her knees. "Yip! Yip-yip!"

Mandy folded arms across her chest and gave the pooch a stern look identical to the one she gave Nolan. "No. En. O."

"Woof!"

She blinked slowly and gritted her teeth.

"He likes you." Nolan stuck a thumb in his jeans pocket and flashed a dashing smile. "And if your mom ends up staying with you, or you need to stay with your mom, I'll keep him."

"What about when you get called on a mission or training?"

"Already spoke with Miss Ivy about helping you out if I'm unavailable."

"She's seventy years old! Besides, you should have asked me first."

"A-n-d you would have said—"

"No."

"C'mon, Mandy. He'll be good for you."

She sighed and eyed the dog. Something in her face softened. "I said no." But enough of a pause remained to let him know he and the dog were making headway here.

The dog yipped and spun round and round before jumping back to face her. His entire body wagged.

Her finger jabbed out in mock scolding. "Cutesy little tricks will get you nowhere." She whirled on Nolan. "You either."

Mooch raised and pressed paws to her knee.

"Like he can understand what I'm saying." Her hand rose and fell against her thigh with a light smack.

The dog gave a soulful whine and stretched his neck playfully until his snout nudged Mandy's fingers.

"His heart's melting." *So is hers.* "He's falling more in love with you by the minute." Nolan dropped his voice and let his gaze linger, hoping she'd get the hint that he had that in common with the dog.

"How can you know that?" Her eyes narrowed into suspicious slits. But she knelt.

He gestured. "Look, his tail is about to wag off and take him airborne."

The St. Bernard emitted another soulful whine and his entire body trembled in yearning.

Nolan chuckled. "See? Besides, I already paid for him."

"Then *you* can take him home with you."

"That was Plan B. But I wanted you to have first dibs on him." He tried to mimic the dog's wide puppy eyes.

An overdrawn sigh blew out of Mandy. "If you're trying to be irresistible, it's not happening." She stood.

One more throaty canine whine.

"You either," she said to the dog. But her good hand snaked down and unceremoniously scrubbed behind overly fluffy ears.

Mooch stepped tentatively toward her and sniffed her arm, then leaped up and licked her nose.

"Ew! Buster used to do that gross nose-licking thing." Momentary hurt flashed over her face and Nolan knew she was remembering. She knelt and wrapped her arm around the dog. He leaned into her. Mandy looked a moment like her impervious resolve would crumble. Hands kneading either side of Mooch's head, she scrubbed beneath his ears.

He wiggled forward and licked her chin. Would have gotten her mouth but she averted her head just in time. Mandy let out a long-suffering sigh. "If you want to be adopted, one thing you need to learn not to do is slime people's faces. Think you can work on that?"

Mooch licked her hand.

"Okay. That's better." She wiped her face with her sleeve. "You'll make someone a great pet. But I have absolutely no business getting one at this point in time." She gave the dog a quick parting hug. Lifted her chin and eyed Nolan with decided finality. "I'm afraid the answer will have to be no."

"So, you're taking me to Refuge Pet Palace on the way home, right? After all, he'll need food and a kennel to sleep in at night."

Nolan grinned, a disgusting look of giddy victory smeared over the imp's face. "Yep. They have heavier bowls and bigger bags of dog food than regular stores."

"Figured as much."

When she'd been adamant with her final "no" she'd expected Nolan's jaw to tense. But he'd only smiled. That incorrigibly optimistic smile he always used to have when he wanted his way and knew he'd eventually get it.

Mandy eyed the dog, facing the back truck window, and shook her head in disbelief. "Now, once again, how did we go to town for a mocha and come back with a mutt? Not to mention one who will eat me out of house and home?"

Nolan laughed. Try as she might to resist its charm, she couldn't. A grin dawned and it felt *good*.

When he caught sight of her smile, his widened like seeing it was the essence of joy. "I'll buy his food for as long as you'll let me." A deeper question embedded his words.

She had no idea what to say to that. How long would they be in each other's lives before he disappeared again?

Oh, no—no—no. She'd gone and gotten attached to Nolan and his loyal ways again. Gotten comfortable with him being around. Too comfortable.

Just like the first time.

Panic welled.

Nolan must have sensed her anxiety because his hand came to rest on her shoulder. "He'll be therapeutic for you." He offered her a sincere expression.

"And that means…"

He shifted uncomfortably. "Mandy, I've noticed lately you don't seem like yourself. It's more than the collapse. As a health care provider, I know you're trained for disasters. Same as I was during paramedic training on the PJ pipeline. Something's off."

"You haven't seen me in ten years. How can you even say that? You don't know me at all. Not the new me."

"You're still you and I know you more than you think."

She sat straighter. "How?" Had he checked up on her without her having known it?

"Because I never stopped thinking about you."

She had to concentrate to keep from aspirating her mint.

"I am concerned you're exhibiting signs of Post Traumatic Stress Disorder."

No. Her stomach hollowed. She couldn't have that. Just, couldn't. Frustration surged. "I haven't just come off a bloody war like those combat-weary soldiers you screen, Nolan."

"*No,* but you have been through a traumatic experience. Saw a lot of people die in one day in an accident so horrific it sent an entire town into mourning."

"You act as though it was cataclysmic. It was just a small-town bridge collapse. I'll get over it."

"Maybe so. But you'll get over it a lot faster with help."

"You saying I need a psychiatrist?"

"Nope. You always did like to put words in my mouth." He grinned. "But I would suggest counseling. I can hook you up with someone at the center where I—"

"No."

"It's the only counseling center in town."

"That's not why I said no. It wouldn't bother me if you were there."

His careful expression said he didn't buy that. "You can't go on like this with lack of quality sleep."

"I appreciate your concern." She reached back and petted the dog lounged in the backseat. He licked her outstretched hand before returning to watch trees and houses scroll by the car window.

Maybe she'd call Amelia and talk to her about it when she got home. They'd been having daily conversations since she'd left the hospital.

"What's the big deal, Mandy? Needing help isn't a stigma."

"I don't need a psych consult while in residency. That goes on my records. I might lose my fellowship at Refuge Memorial and not be able to take the boards." She pressed fingers into her throbbing temples. "Surely this is temporary stress." It would go away after images of the collapse faded.

Yet what about the return of Nolan and the hurts that evoked?

The only way to alleviate that and prevent a recurrence would be to stay away from him. Relocating wasn't an option. Being around him drew her back to him emotionally. Like turning the magnet.

Well, that simply wouldn't do. She needed to be more careful. Guard her emotions and heart. The only way to do that would be to avoid him. But how? He seemed entrenched in her life again.

And just how had that happened?

Now at the pet store, he shut off the ignition and put the leash on Mooch. "Come on, boy."

Mandy followed with a sense of aggravation gnawing her. Suspicion mounted as to his motive. Nolan always used to make decisions for her. The main one being their parting the way they did, which hurt like nothing she'd ever known.

As they traipsed the pet store aisles, she battled outrage as she studied him.

Did he know the effect he was having on her? Is that why he got her the dog and asked her to go to the park with him next week? To ensure another way to stay in her life, in hopes they would reattach emotionally?

As if feeling her stare, he met it briefly. "If you decide to see a counselor I can hook you up with a great one who will probably give you a discount if money's a—"

"I'll be fine, Nolan. End of subject."

If she was going to see a counselor, it would be on her own time and dime. And she'd travel to another town if need be.

Time to start snipping the stealthy thread that had slipped in and begun weaving their lives—and hearts—back together. A gram of pain now was better than a liter of it later.

Chapter Ten

"Picnic table or grass?" Nolan asked days later while walking the dog across the lush grounds of Haven Street Park.

She eyed the table but gestured toward the blanket. "Grass will be fine. That way Mooch can sit with us."

With a grand sweep of the blanket, Nolan spread it over freshly-cut grass. That aroma mingled with a woodsy soap scent as Nolan bent to help Mandy sit. Mooch immediately found a spot next to her and snuggled himself close.

Nolan bit an inch out of his Italian sub. "You've hardly touched yours."

"What?" Mandy felt especially dazed today. The lack of sleep was making her feel older than Miss Ivy.

"Better eat before it gets cold."

"I don't have an appetite."

"You should take the meds with food."

"I'd rather tough the pain out than eat that. I'm not all that fond of Italian subs nowadays. Besides, you keep doing this."

"What?"

"Reminding me of the past in subtle ways. Taking me places like we always used to go. Bringing me things that we always used to like to share." And it was making her fall hard and fast all over again. She wished she could let go of the fear they'd have to separate and just enjoy his courtship.

To his credit, he looked genuinely confused. "Like what?"

"Like breakfast burritos and Italian subs. Not to mention the dog…that you say is mine yet you decided to name because you still have a tendency to want to make people's decisions for them."

He blinked. Lowered his sandwich and appeared to chew on her words instead.

"That sets up red flags in me, Nolan. I don't like how you're trying to infiltrate yourself back into my life and heart." She set her sub aside.

"I wasn't consciously doing that. I knew they used to be your favorite food, so I was trying to be considerate. I apologize if I've seemed too forward."

He went from looking like a scolded child to militantly intent. "But one thing I won't apologize for is trying to get close to you again."

He rose and stuck two fingers into his mouth, whistling at the dog, who must have caught the scent of something. Ears flopped as he conducted a zigzag sprint toward trees.

"Mooch! Here, boy." He tossed the dog the remains of his sandwich, then eyed hers. "Still not gonna eat that?"

She shook her head, tongue tingling to taste the pastrami and spicy salami. But her stomach had felt queasy for days. The last thing she wanted was to be sick in the middle of a public park.

In one fluid motion, he grasped her sandwich and tossed it to the dog. How a man could be bulky and graceful simultaneously, she didn't know. Uncomfortable with this new kind of attraction toward Nolan, she shoved her sunglasses on. Maybe that would block the glare of his gorgeous golden tan.

"You really shouldn't feed human food to dogs. It can make them sick. No wonder you named him Mooch." Her words held more of an edge than she'd intended. Where was that coming from?

Pausing in his athletic, mesmerizing strides, he faced her. "For your information, the dog was already named. I didn't want to confuse him by changing it. He already had a family before you. But they turned around and brought him back after neglecting him for days."

Her heart tugged. "Aww! Poor Mooch."

"That's why I picked him. You always had a tender heart for the ignored and neglected."

Images of Nolan's tough childhood where he hadn't felt like he belonged anywhere besides their friendship zipped to mind.

But Nolan had used his trials and everything life tossed him to reach out to others in need of rescue. Whether emotional or physical. He did it then. And he was doing it now. In his life as a pararescueman, and, she suspected, with her in her current mental state thanks to a bridge disappearance and his reappearance. What an inspiration he was.

He must have mistaken her silence for displeasure because he shoved fingertips through his attractive tough-guy buzz cut that complemented his strong facial bone structure.

He stepped toward her and knelt. "I thought he'd adjust better if we kept his name."

We.

Mandy felt like she'd swallowed both subs whole but Mooch munched on them with canine fervor. Something huge lodged in her throat at the frustrated can't-do-anything-right look on Nolan's face.

Something weighed him down. Something more than her. Yet all she could do was gripe at him. Hadn't he always been there for her?

She started to reach out for him but again, felt frozen. Just as she'd nearly thawed enough, Mooch took off after a squirrel.

With a speed and agility she didn't know a human could

possess, Nolan was on his feet and tearing up grass. He gained on the dog. The man must spend seven hours a day in the gym.

And just so he could go into the thickest kinds of danger in the world's most unforgiving terrain and risk his neck to save people with no idea how hard he trained to better his chances of bringing them back alive.

"I'm sorry," she whispered to Nolan's back, then blinked away uninvited tears that had been terrorizing her along with other various emotional outbursts since the day the road of her perfectly paved world collapsed.

Countless emotions rushed her as she observed him run with Mooch. Genuine, spontaneous giggles consumed her. And it felt *good.* She laughed at the man she couldn't keep her eyes off of. And at her new canine confidant whom she'd come to love even though he squashed her feet beneath covers at night. They frolicked all over the park.

Mandy pushed off the blanket and joined the fun. When Nolan steered them toward the jungle gym, heat flushed her cheeks.

Mandy and Nolan's first kiss had been in a park on a jungle gym when she was fifteen and he sixteen.

Would he remember? She lifted her eyes.

He stared straight at her, with a smug grin on a face that held the bar on handsome. A bold, daring look informed her that, yes, he indeed remembered. She swallowed and strode away. Far away. His chuckle wafted all the way across the park. And if she didn't know better, that silly St. Bernard smiled as well.

As he and Mooch caught up to her, a little boy bounded up, trailed by a Hispanic woman. "Nolan!"

Nolan swung around. "Hey, Celia. Bradley." Nolan tossed a ball for Mooch. "How's Manny?" He walked toward them as they approached.

"Oh, you know. About like the last time he had surgery."

"Being a baby?" Nolan laughed.

"Not so much. He refused to take meds, which makes him grumpy. So Bradley and I decided to play in the park. We were just headed home to fix Manny lunch when we saw you." Celia eyed Mandy with unabashed interest. "Who do we have here?"

"This is the friend I was telling you about."

"Oh, wow!" Blatantly, she looked Mandy up and down. "I can totally see why he's still *Caliente* for you after all these years." She stepped forward smiling. "I'm Celia Péna. You must be Manda Panda."

Mandy's flush matched the Red Delicious apple she nearly dropped at feisty Celia's words. Nolan chomped back a laugh at Mandy's stricken expression. Celia no longer fazed him. He'd grown to love her teasing brashness and goodhearted flair for matchmaking every unattached person she knew.

The possibilities brought a grin to his face. With Celia and God on his side, Mandy didn't stand a chance.

"That your dog?" Bradley asked Mandy.

"Sure. Wanna pet him?" Kneeling, Mandy chuckled. Amazing how she transformed when children were around. She'd loved children as long as Nolan could remember. Even when she was one, she'd help babysit younger kids in the neighborhood.

"Is he an outside dog?" Celia pushed sunglasses over her forehead.

"Inside. If it works out that way. I haven't had him long."

"He's just a puppy, huh?" Bradley grinned and petted the dog.

"And still learning." Mandy yawned.

"You look like the sleepy bug got you." Bradley grinned. Mandy nodded and quelled another yawn. "I am tired."

Bradley rubbed Mooch's chin. "How come?"

She blinked a couple times and tilted her head. Nolan knew she pondered how to answer. Had she been plagued with nightmares again, he doubted she'd tell that to a kid.

"Partly because he slept scrunched on top of my feet last night. No matter how many times I ordered him to stay put in the laundry room, he kept coming back to my room. Next thing I know, my blankets are disturbed and this incredibly cold nose is sniffing my feet."

Celia laughed and brushed a hand along Bradley's head. "We better *vamoose*. Manny will be a grumpy bear without his lunch." Celia spun to go but flounced back around. "So, Nolan—now I know why you've been MIA at the Friday night gigs." Celia slung a pointed look at Mandy, winked and waved goodbye in a grandiose arm gesture, smirking all the while.

"Hey," Nolan called, jogging to her. "When's Joel get back?"

"Week or so."

After walking Celia and Bradley to the car, Nolan returned. "That's one of my teammates' wives. Bradley is the son of my team leader, Joel."

"He's cute. How old is he?"

"Ten, I think."

"Wow. He looks younger." Her brow pinched with concern.

"He's well now, but a couple years ago, they nearly lost him to leukemia."

Her eyes widened. "He's small, but looks normal and healthy."

"He is. Bradley's also the bravest person I know."

Mandy stared after them with compassion. "Is he in remission now?"

"Yeah. Has been since a bone marrow transplant."

"Oh, good. I'm glad he got one and that it was successful."

"Me, too. He's basically the reason our team ended up based in Refuge. Come to think of it, he started it all."

"How so?"

"He was in foster care and given only so long to live. He wished to meet the special ops airman who grew up here. That was Joel."

"He's not his biological dad?"

Nolan shook his head. "Bradley's teacher adopted him and Joel free-fell head over for both of them."

Emotion glitzed Mandy's eyes. "That is an amazing story. I love happy endings."

"It didn't stop there. Manny started dating Celia, who was co teaching Bradley's class with Amber, Bradley's adoptive mother. They married and Manny adopted Celia's teenage son, Javier. His dad was a Refuge police officer, killed in the line of duty."

"Goodness." Mandy pulled her feet under her.

"We never thought Manny and Celia would get together. But they're deliriously happy now. With so many of the PJs settling here, Joel had the home base transferred to Eagle Point, Refuge Air Base. Then Ben met a girl who was passing through town and they're about to be married."

Mandy wiggled as if something prickled over her. "Ben. have heard that name on another occasion." A strange look of dread and wonder crossed her face.

"Maybe on the bridge? There's a Ben on my team."

"Probably a different one then." Doubt clouded her features, recriminating her words. She plucked stray fiber from the picnic blanket. "I have a hard time believing that you're not married, Nolan."

Nolan's throat tightened. He'd wanted a family for so long but... "I have my reasons." The main one being no woman had ever measured up to the one sitting right in front of him.

"You mentioned yesterday you're training at the counsel ing center?" Mandy bit into her apple.

It was good to see her eating. She'd dropped weight since the collapse. Another concerning sign.

Nolan poured water from the cooler in a bowl for Mooch. "I'm taking classes to get a counseling certificate. It's going to become part of a program we're developing to try and keep me on the team."

Lapping sounded as Mooch siphoned the water.

"I remember you mentioned you might be disbanded from your team. I'm sorry, Nolan." She nibbled her lip.

Her sincerity touched him. "Hopefully there'll be no reason to mourn. If we develop the program to brass specifications, I'll have a better shot at thwarting my reassignment."

The words seemed to startle her a moment and he instinctually knew her mind flashed back to their breakup a decade ago.

Time for a change in subject. He wanted to talk to her about it, but not until her mind was clear and her body rested with adequate sleep. It could be a few weeks, but a conversation that important could wait until the optimal time.

"How's Mooch adjusting?"

A laugh scraped from Mandy. "Well, the first night I figured out he's scared of the dryer. He chewed and ripped a basket of my jeans to shreds. The pants all looked like they'd exploded. Then he repeatedly body slammed the laundry room door, which he'd clawed the paint off of, until I let him out."

"Ah, poor guy." Nolan scratched Mooch's chin.

Arms holding her knees, she rocked back. "Why a counselor?"

"One, there's a need for it. Two, because so many soldiers are coming back from deployment with PTSD. That'll be my specialty. I'll form a post-combat screening and treatment program and run it out of Refuge Air Base. I also hope to provide marriage counseling to deployed soldiers with families."

"Hmm. Wouldn't they want someone who's been married?" She gulped and swallowed as if her tea went down hard. "I—I'm sorry if you've been married, Nolan. I had no business saying that."

He set down his soda. "I never married. And the marital counseling thing wasn't my idea. Joel and Petrowski asked me to because I have compassion for couples separated by deployment."

"You'll be good at it. You've always been compassionate, wise, and caring."

He studied her carefully. "Except when I left you standing on that bus corner," Nolan said after they'd eaten.

His bluntness slapped a look of shock on her face. But some things needed to be said. On the other hand, he sensed he needed to tread lightly and listen for God's cues.

Nolan rose. "Come on, Mandy. Let's take Mooch for a walk." After Mooch walked them all over the park, Nolan eyed his watch. He needed to meet Petrowski at the DZ to fortify continued plans to keep himself on the team. Superiors had given them an extension on their deadline since Joel was out of the country.

"I had a nice time," Mandy said as he helped her out of the car with the dog at Ivy Manor.

"I'll walk you in."

"Would you like to stay for coffee?"

His heart sagged. The one time she actually invited him into her apartment, and he had a meeting. But his future with the team hinged on it.

He walked her slowly to the door, wanting to draw out their time to the last possible second. "Mandy, you have no idea how much I'd love to stay. But I've got a meeting I can't miss."

At her door now, she tilted her face up and time stood still. He hovered close. How badly he wanted to kiss her. She must have known because her gaze dropped to his lips, too. He inclined his head, drowning in her knockout eyes. They fluttered as she swayed into him.

The dog yipped.

Mandy gasped. A look of sheer fright crossed her features.

Talk about being yanked from a slow-motion trance by a high-speed dog.

A groan gritted Nolan's teeth. He needed to have a one-on-one talk with that interfering mutt.

Nolan reached for her. "Mandy, I—"

She spun, all but clawing for the door and shoving the dog inside with her knee. She made self-deprecating groans and rapid blinks and if he weren't mistaken, her breathing was soaring out of normal limits.

From heady enchantment associated with the near-miss-kiss? Or something else? She had that fight-or-flight thing going on. He hoped it wouldn't trigger a bridge flashback.

He stuck his foot in her door. "Wait, Mandy—"

"You need to go. Goodbye, Nolan."

With reluctance, he pulled his foot from the crack.

The door slam matched the resolve of permanence in her parting tone. *Goodbye, Nolan.*

He pressed one hand to the door and one to his chest and wondered which walls were closing in faster. Either way, the thought of never seeing her again threatened to steal his air.

"I don't want there to be another permanent goodbye between us," he whispered to her door and pressed his hand harder on the wood. "She's worth fighting for. But so is my team. God help me do both."

It hit Nolan like a two-ton mortar. He hadn't felt this way until he'd seen Mandy again. Before the bridge collapse, he wouldn't have been able to name one thing save God that could compete with his love and devotion to his team.

The thought that she might just be a distraction nearly sent him to his knees right there in the hallway.

"I never would have said this a few weeks ago. But I want them equally. Please don't make me choose between them again."

But what if he had to? What would he do?

Nolan forced himself to walk back to his truck.

What if he had to? What would he do?

He lived his life by his pararescue creed. Not even marriage could compete with that. If his military placement were the only thing he had to lose, there'd be no question. But he'd promised Chief Petrowski he'd go.

Maybe he shouldn't try to win Mandy back because his feelings for her could compete with his promise. Besides, it wasn't like she'd even given him the option.

And another thing stacked against them was that her heart hadn't yet turned back to God. Nor Nolan in a romantic sense.

But if both of those things happened, what would he do? How would he choose? Unless she became willing to give up her dreams of staying in one place and building a pediatric practice and free health clinics for children…

They were right back to square one.

The same dusty, cracked concrete square they stood on ten years ago, crying and clinging to one another for a goodbye he never meant to last a decade.

If his deepest dreams came true with Mandy and his two most uttered prayers were answered, it could be the worst thing possible for his career. He'd pledged allegiance to go where he was needed. Which would he choose? Mandy? Or his career?

Sweat broke out over his palms at the dreaded answer.

"It might have been better had we never seen each other again. Reunion Bridge, God? How ironic. If You'd like to clue me in, I'd love nothing more than to know what on earth You are doing."

Chapter Eleven

Mandy's phone chimed a classic rock tune the next morning.

She stumbled into the kitchen and tripped over a heap on her way there. It lifted its head and yelped. Not sure which came first. "Sorry, Mooch." She turned on the lamp and flipped open her cell, charging on the counter.

Amelia's name on the ID put her instantly awake. "Hey!"

"Hi, it's me again."

"Hi, me."

"Hope I'm not bugging you."

"Never."

"You sound groggy. Did I wake you?"

"Uh, maybe a little. But that's okay. I needed to get up. I have a doctor's appointment today. One month since surgery."

"Need a ride?"

"Sure, if you can swing it." Mandy was pretty sure Nolan had meetings on Tuesday mornings. And her lack of sleep had caused her to forget to secure a ride.

"Absolutely. Also wondered if you want to go have coffee with me again this morning?"

"I'll never say no to great coffee, or great company."

"Yay! See you at nine." Even through the phone line,

Mandy felt a warmth from Amelia North that reached out and beckoned for a long and lasting friendship. A best-friend kind of friendship. Mandy knew the importance of having close female friends and a support system.

Mandy hated being alone, period, much less in a new town with no friends. At some point it had become very important to befriend Amelia. That they were becoming fast friends in such a short amount of time had to be a God thing, right?

A God thing.

How long had it been since that phrase had entered the vocabulary of her heart?

Maybe reading the Bible Nolan left here was helping. Not that she'd readily admit that to him quite yet.

Speaking of the Bible, if he left his copy here with her, what was *he* reading? She determined to drill him about that one.

Hope surged in Mandy that concern for people's faith in God would once again come to life in her heart. All it would take was one breath of God to bring her faith alive again. No matter how far gone or how long.

So much of her younger years had been spent praying over others. Laboring in prayer for her friends' or family members' lost or failing faith.

Never in those days would she have dreamed she'd be the one in need of those prayers.

But who would pray for her like she'd prayed for others?

Nolan.

She clutched his Bible to her chest, though it was a tangible echo of the faith that she had prayed he'd one day embrace, she hadn't been able to read it again until now. Something fluttered from beneath it. Her take-home instruction sheet from the hospital, and…something in Nolan's handwriting. Funny how she remembered it all these years.

Slowly, she read it. Then again, and his words both moved

and sobered her. She bent forward and broke, sobbing. Shooed Mooch away as he incessantly licked tears from her face.

Then she started laughing as she rubbed the dog's head. "You probably don't have sympathy as much as you have a penchant for salt, huh boy?"

No matter. The best was true. She had the gift of Nolan's prayers. Mandy rose to wash her face. She suspected Amelia prayed for her, too. Soon, a car pulling up outside drew her toward the door.

"Where's Reece?" Mandy let Amelia inside.

"School. Then she had GiGs afterward."

Mandy yawned. "Remind me what GiGs is again?"

"Girlfriends in God. Sort of like a faith-based Girl Scouts."

"Ah. You might have mentioned that."

"Sistahchick, you are spacey. I've told you like three times in the past two weeks what GiGs is. Sure you don't need to just crawl back into bed?" Concern laced her jovial voice as she scanned Mandy's attire of pajamas and a fluffy bathrobe.

Another yawn accosted Mandy. "Nope. Once I'm awake, I'm awake for the day. Plus, I can't miss my doctor's appointment."

"I won't call so early next time. I think you need sleep more than coffee."

Mandy laughed and tugged an outfit from her closet and headed to the bathroom for a quick shower. "I plan to remedy that today at the doctor's office. He'll order something to help me sleep better. I'd still love to grab coffee beforehand."

Amelia bent to pet Mooch. "I hope the sleep aid takes care of whatever's causing this insomnia."

Nolan's voice wafted across Mandy's mind like silent ticker tape: *Post Traumatic Stress Disorder. Medication may not be enough. I think you may need to see a counselor…*

"Me, too."

* * *

"Something's terribly wrong," Mandy said, as they pulled back up to Ivy Manor after her appointment. Her mom, who must have flown back in, looked worse than before. She sat on the steps with tissues strewn about her.

"Who is that?" Amelia asked.

"My mom. Please pray. I have a sick feeling." She flung open the door and ran toward Marva. Amelia trailed.

Marva rose. "Hi, Mandy."

"Mom, what's going on? You look terrible."

She choked out a laugh. "I feel terrible, too. Who's your friend?"

"I'm Amelia. Should I leave?" She looked from Mandy to Marva.

Mandy grabbed her arm knowing she'd need her support if this was more bad news. "No. Please don't." She faced her mom. "Let's go inside."

Once seated, Marva plucked at tissues again. Her hands, Mandy noticed, were blue-black. "You've had lots of lab work lately."

Marva nodded. "Tests."

"For?" Mandy's heart fisted her sternum.

Marva looked up. "Mandy, I have cancer."

Mandy drew a breath but didn't feel like she got air. "Where?"

Rocking, Marva rested her hands on her abdomen. "Ovarian."

Mandy reached forward and held her mom's arms. "How bad?"

Marva sniffed. "I don't know yet. I have more tests next week."

"I'll come with you."

Marva laughed. "No, actually, I'd rather you didn't."

"You sure?"

She rocked again but looked Mandy eye to eye. "Yes. I'll call you as soon as I know something."

"I'd rather be with you."

Marva's cheeks tinged. "I'd rather you didn't."

Mandy wanted to scream. "Mom, you don't have to suffer alone."

Amelia smiled. Then covered her mouth.

"What?" Mandy asked her.

"Seems she passed those stubborn genes on to you."

The women shared a lighthearted laugh but it didn't diminish the uncertainty cloaking the room. It put another layer of weight on Mandy's already sagging shoulders.

"Can I stay with you for a few days?" Marva asked.

"Uh, of course. But you should know I have a dog. And that Nolan's been coming over regularly."

Marva shrugged but it seemed more like a bristle. "Suit yourself."

Great. Just when Mandy was starting to be able to let herself enjoy Nolan's company, this barrier comes. Who knew whether Nolan'd stick around for the long haul?

Maybe her mom being here was a blessing in disguise, keeping her from getting too emotionally close to either of them.

But what of the small chance he would remain in her life for its duration now? Marva wouldn't be happy about it.

Mandy didn't know what she'd do. Not at all. Not about any of this.

A knock drew Mandy out of bed the next day. She threw on her robe and pattered to the door feeling woozy still from the sleeping pill. Thankfully the guest room, Marva's door, was still closed so the knocking must not have woken her. The tile felt chilly on her bare feet. Where was Mooch? Probably snuck in with her mom. Mandy laughed about that. She unlocked the door.

Nolan stood on the other side.

Suppressing the urge to sneak him in and hide him, she let him in, then paused. "Wait. Were you here earlier this morning?"

He chuckled. "Yeah. But you were out of it. Glad to know you weren't too tired to lock your door. Although I've been knocking for five minutes." His eyes did a leisurely stroll from her face to her bare pink toes and back. That's when she noticed he had her dog on the end of a leash. Obviously Nolan walked him.

"I must have slept like a mummy in a coma." She pulled her robe tighter and eyed Marva's door where shuffling sounded.

Great. She's awake.

Nolan grinned and handed her the cup of coffee he brought her each morning. "I guess. You assaulted the alarm clock this morning." Nolan unhooked the collar from the leash.

"I did?" Mandy stepped aside as Mooch bounded past, ready to upend anything in his boisterous-puppy path.

"Yeah. Smacked the snooze button four times before leaning over and jerking the cord out of the wall. I know because you slept with your door open."

She laughed then stuttered. "But, my clock has a battery backup."

It felt good to laugh with Nolan. But as soon as Marva got up, that would be the end of that. "Wait, how did you get in?"

"Miss Ivy. She was scared to come check on you by herself, when you hadn't risen at your normal time." Hands plunged in his pocket, they emerged and opened. Two double-A batteries appeared in his palms. "Not anymore. I figured you needed your rest and took them out."

She shook her head. "I can't sleep the day away."

"Yes, you can. I'm glad you finally found a sleep aid that's helping you actually sleep."

"I sleep, yes but it makes the nightmares worse, which makes me shake." Either way, sleep or no sleep, she felt depressed, anxious and on the verge of a panic attack all day.

If she told him though, he'd just bug her about counseling. "Where'd you go?" Not that it mattered. No idea why she even asked.

"To a meeting and then for a run. With your dog."

"I see that." Nodding, she rubbed her arms and moved toward the thermostat. He set out their breakfast, just as he did every time he came over. Whoops. None for Marva. Should she tell Nolan her mom was here? And about the cancer?

Mandy's appetite fled. "Be proud. I took your advice and have been having coffee with a friend."

He nodded. "I'm glad you're getting out some. Wouldn't want you to become agoraphobic on top of suffering PTSD." He grinned.

She whacked him with the newspaper he'd brought her from the hall. "I do not have PTSD."

He leveled her with a look that needed no words to convince her of his refuting that statement.

She spun away. "You think you know everything."

He paused. "I don't claim to know everything. But I do know the signs of PTSD. You have most of them and more."

"You think I don't know what they are? It's just simple stress that will go away."

"When?"

"Sooner or later." She rubbed her arms feeling caged.

"It'd be sooner if you'll consider counseling."

She sighed. "We've been through this."

"Yeah, a dozen times. Only I don't understand why you're being so obstinate about it."

He was right. She'd avoided the idea of counseling like the end of a needle.

Tell him.

Panic thumped her heart against her chest until she focused on taking deep breaths. Enough to be able to say what she needed to.

"Nolan, the bridge collapse isn't the only thing upsetting me."

He paused and turned slowly.

She took another breath. "You may not believe this but I'm actually a very emotionally stable person."

He grinned. "Wait, wait. Now hold on. I never thought you were emotionally unstable. You were a teenage girl suffering from hormones and your parents' break-up."

"Well, when you put it like that, yes. I was emotionally volatile. And weak. I'm not that person anymore. At least, I wasn't until the day of the collapse."

"I never thought of you as weak, Mandy." He came close and caressed her face with his hand and her heart with his words. "I thought of you then how I think of you now."

"How?"

"You're smart. Capable. Brave. Courageous. Caring. Beautiful. Strong. Gorgeous. Honest."

"Nolan, you're part of the reason I can't sleep at night."

"Uh, that should make me feel better, except that you look about to cry. Or punch me." He backed up a step.

"Not funny."

He reached a hand to her cheek.

She tilted her face away from his touch lest she give in and shrink back from what she needed to do. "No, Nolan. I mean, you resurfaced old hurts. From a long time ago that I didn't realize were still there. I've had more nightmares about the way we parted than about the bridge."

He led her to the couch. "There's more."

She nodded, feeling her throat close. "Mom's here. She has cancer." She paused to let him take that in.

He sighed. "Mandy, I'm sorry."

And Mandy wanted to explore a relationship with Nolan. But her mom was sick and every outcome seemed uncertain. "I'm ripped up about it."

How had her voice turned so mean and grating and why couldn't she control these emotional outbursts?

In fact, Nolan looked stricken. He swallowed. "Mandy, I'm sorry. I had no idea—"

"Of course you wouldn't. You had no idea then how much my heart was breaking either. And then when you didn't call—"

"I did." His jaw tensed.

"When? Please don't lie to me." She quelled the overpowering urge to fling up her arms in frustration. Never had she this much trouble with control.

"I've never lied to you." Nolan flicked a glance toward the guestroom door. Why?

"Yes, you have. You promised to call and you never did. Had no intention of doing so."

"Mandy, I did. I—" He clamped his mouth shut.

He what? She clutched at his shirt. "Nolan, tell me."

"Never mind. I shouldn't have dumped over this pail of pythons." He shook his head. "Leave it be, Mandy." It came out a low growl. Like Mooch when someone passed her door outside the hall. He rose, pent up energy propelling him to pace.

She pursued him around the table. "I can't."

"I won't hurt you further. Don't revisit it."

"If you won't talk about it and tell me the truth, then I won't see you again." She stalked toward the door. Felt like cursing but she held the sounds at bay. Was the PTSD making her act this way?

"I don't want to leave."

"You have to." She needed all her energy in order to overcome the trauma from the collapse and regain control over her emotions. She didn't need his influence and certainly not this sudden turn of uncovered events hanging over her.

Yanking the door open, she pointed toward the hall. "Go.

I don't want to see you again. Or talk to you. Goodbye. And this time, I mean it for good."

"You're being ridiculous."

Her mouth dropped open. "No, I'm doing what it takes."

"To hide."

"To survive."

"There's no way we'll not run into each other. Least we can do is learn to be civil."

"Let's learn to avoid one another as much as possible and keep our eyes on our prizes."

That apparently ticked him off because his jaw rhythmically clicked. "And your prize would be?"

"Being a doctor, right here in one town for life. As yours would be flying on the wings of pararescue and wherever that blows you. You're meant to be a rescuer, Nolan. Just not for me."

Frustration skittered across the surface of his deeply discerning eyes. "He brought us back together. Are you too blind from bitterness to see?"

"All I see is that you are trespassing. And that we coincidentally ran into each other."

"I'll bet that felt like a slap to His face, Mandy. He's given us another chance to be together."

"Nolan, I can't stand to be around you."

Now, Nolan looked slapped and she knew he took it the wrong way. Then his face softened. "I can't stand the thought of being without you. And neither can God. I guarantee He won't obey if you ask him to stay away. And you'd better be glad for that. But if you're ordering me to, I will. I won't like it. But I'll comply. But only because I have enough self-respect not to want to be arrested by Stallings for stalking."

Drat, she nearly laughed at that but held her ground. "Fine. Please leave."

"Mandy—"

"Goodbye, Nolan.

"We have to co-exist in the same town. I don't want things to be weird between us."

"Things will always be weird between us. It's nothing I can't handle." Something inside whispered, *"Liar."*

"I didn't mean to hurt you back then."

She shrugged. "You broke my heart but I'm over it now." But even as her mouth released the words, her heart knew it wasn't true. "I've moved on, but that doesn't mean I want to torture myself by dredging up old memories and revisiting hurts."

"I'm sorry I hurt you, Mandy. That's the last thing I wanted. And I don't want to hurt you now."

"Then, please. Do both of us a favor, Nolan. Stay away from me. If you really want to help me, that's what you'll do."

He stood very still, then stepped backward off the porch. Turned without another word and left.

Chapter Twelve

Two-week-long tension gripped Nolan's neck muscles. Tension from missing Mandy. He growled in frustration when his climbing gear tangled.

"Dude, what is up with you? You haven't cracked a smile for days." Brock swiped sweat and grime from his eyes.

"I'm in a bad mood." Nolan tossed rappelling gear on top of the cliff his team was about to perform another training operation on. They'd paired off in twos along the bluff.

"How's Mandy?" Brock asked pointedly.

Nolan shrugged. "I wouldn't know." He'd respected her wishes and left her alone.

"You guys still not talking?" Brock rigged his rope clasp.

Nolan shook his head and strapped sandbags to a basket they were to "rescue" from the side of a remote bluff. "I miss her."

Brock laughed. "You should go to Wal-Mart, then."

"Why's that?" Nolan double-checked his rappelling rig.

"Every time I go to Wal-Mart, I see someone I know. Maybe you'd see Mandy."

"Maybe." Nolan stepped to the edge of the bluff precipice and held the rope. "But for now, we're gonna rescue a bunch of sandbags." He'd put Mandy out of his mind, and focused on his job training.

Nolan signaled to those below, then stepped over the edge of one of Refuge's best rocky cliffs.

Two weeks and ten Wal-Mart trips later, Nolan nearly lost his willpower and called her. Missing her hurt him, but he'd been through worse.

He yanked open his door at Refuge Bed and Breakfast where his unmarried teammates rented units. He jogged down the boardwalk to Brock's apartment.

"Hey, Briggs." Brock opened the door and stepped aside. "What's up?"

Nolan hiked a thumb toward his truck. "Let's go back to Wal-Mart. I'm out of batteries for my flashlight."

Brock smirked. "You got some last week."

"I might be out of trash bags."

"There's a full box of white ones under your sink."

"Then I'll exchange it."

"Trash bags?" But Brock grabbed his wallet off the counter. Nolan nodded.

"For what?"

"Box of black ones."

Brock followed him to the truck. "You're bad. But hey, Wal-Mart's always an adventure. Some of the strangest people show up there."

Nolan laughed and turned the key in the ignition. "Then what does that say about us, having gone there almost every day for two weeks?" They'd gone around visiting wind tunnels, too. But in between those out-of-the-area research trips, Nolan spent every spare minute perusing store aisles for a familiar face.

"Thought you were trying to avoid her?"

"I am. I'm also out of V8 Juice."

"You don't drink that stuff, dude."

No, but Mandy did. And, in faith, he'd buy a six pack to keep around…just in case his prayers were answered and she came around.

At ten to nine Mandy tightened her sling and stared out her window at the parking lot of Ivy Manor with an anticipation she'd not felt in a while. She'd grown to look forward to coffee time with Amelia on Tuesdays.

An instant smile tugged her mouth when Amelia pulled up and parked in front of the curb. She hadn't realized how much she'd been missing female friendships.

Nor had she realized how bad she'd miss Nolan because he'd actually listened to her ridiculous rant and stayed away.

No phone calls. No visits. Nothing.

But that's what she'd wanted, right?

She scratched Mooch on his head and checked to be sure he had fresh food and water. "Why do I always act opposite of how I feel, huh buddy?"

But she honestly thought it would even out her emotions to not be around Nolan.

The last three weeks of no contact had proved her painfully wrong. She'd been having more nightmares than usual to the point she didn't even want to sleep. Having left after staying a week, her mom hadn't been back nor called. Hopefully no news was good news, right? Marva hadn't returned Mandy's calls.

"Grrr!" Why did there have to be goodbyes?

Mooch followed her to the door and whined. "Miss Ivy is coming to take you as soon as she gets out of the shower." Not that the dog would understand a word of what she just said.

But the poor shaggy beast of a pup looked so forlorn at her leaving without him, it made Mandy feel better to say it. She knew too well what loneliness felt like.

Purse slung over the shoulder of her good arm, she pushed open the front door and stepped into sunshine.

Amelia greeted her with a smile.

"Hi, princess!" Mandy waved to Reece as she lowered herself in the car.

Reece returned the wave. "Good to see you, Miss Mandy. I missed you since last week." Reece pointed to her teddy bear. "So did Bearby."

Silly as it was, Mandy found herself waving to the toy just to see Reece smile. "Hi, Bearby. You missed me too?"

"Yes, and so did Mommy," Reece announced.

"It's true. We did," Amelia said, voice quivery.

Amelia must have noticed because her smile faded and she clutched Mandy's arms. "Are you okay?"

I miss Nolan.

Mandy shrugged and smiled. "Yeah. I don't know what on earth is wrong with me. I've felt volatile since the collapse." Mandy eyed Reece and said discreetly, "How is she doing?"

"Seems to be fine. Hasn't had any nightmares or anything. But she also doesn't know some people never made it off the bridge."

"I don't blame you for not telling her."

"So what about you? How have you been sleeping since the new pills?" Now at the town square, Amelia held the seat forward so Reece could exit.

"Terribly. I can hardly go an hour without awful images of the bridge giving way coming to my mind. I hope it gets better soon because I'm starting to feel spacey and exhausted from lack of sleep."

"Feel? You look it, too."

Mandy shared a laugh with her new friend as they walked to the building together. Last night when she had called to confirm they were still getting together today, they'd stayed on the phone for hours, like teenagers, giggling and talking about Amelia's wedding preparations.

Speaking of…Amelia's face sparkled like her diamond.

Once seated, Mandy reached in and tilted Amelia's ring finger to the light. "Wow. It's so pretty, all I want to do is look at it!" Longing to have her own engagement ring, Nolan's face traipsed through her mind.

She dropped Amelia's hand.

Genuine happiness for her friend gushed back. "How did you meet him?"

Amelia laughed. "I literally don't remember."

Mandy's brows rose as they found a table inside the coffee shop, which smelled heavenly. All sorts of rich aromas wafted around them.

"I was unconscious. They tell me he saved my life."

"For real?"

Amelia nodded. "That's why Reece is afraid of hospitals. Refuge at least. I was there almost a week with an electrolyte imbalance."

"Wow." Thankfulness washed through her that Amelia survived. Electrolyte imbalances were life-threatening. "I'm glad you're here."

"Me, too. I would have missed out of so much, including meeting you."

"I feel the same way! I look forward to Tuesdays.

"How are the wedding plans coming?" Mandy asked after they'd put in their coffee orders at the counter and received the warm brew. Reece had taken three quick sips of her kiddy cocoa shake and ran for the Plexiglas-encased play area, visible from where Mandy and Amelia sat.

So Amelia felt it, too. The pull of a friendship meant to happen.

"Thank You." Mandy didn't know why God was being so kind to her when she hadn't kept up communication with Him until the bridge collapse. But somehow she knew this friendship with Amelia was an extension of God's out-stretched hand.

Could it be possible that God would just forget all the

years her love for Him had been desolate? How could God be so forgiving as to hand-gather the parts of a faith fractured like glass and lovingly piece it back together?

Like the chasm never happened.

She thought of Nolan. And how badly she'd wanted him to "get it" growing up. Then she thought of what she and Nolan had but couldn't continue due to his enlisting and continual rejection of her faith. Now look who was running from the divine pursuer?

The road back looks so long...

Reece skipped back to the table. "Mommy, can we now?"

Mandy looked from mother to daughter, who both turned to her. Reece giggled.

Amelia pulled open her purse. "She has something for you."

Reece grinned and pulled out a strip of rhinestone stickers.

Mandy laughed. "For me?"

"Yep. Now you will have a diva cast," Reece announced.

Amelia's eyes twinkled. "She used her allowance to purchase those."

"You bought them for me yourself?" Mandy asked Reece.

"Yup." Reece darted forward and hugged Mandy.

Mandy reciprocated. "Thank you, sweetie! Since I only have one working hand, can you help me put them on?"

One by one Reece peeled the rhinestone stickers and affixed them in various places along the cast. "Now, it's pretty," she proclaimed with a little person voice and a big person nod. "Mommy, can I go play some more?"

Amelia nodded and Reece sped off.

"What do you have planned the rest of the week?" Amelia asked after they'd finished their lattes and returned to Ivy Manor.

"Nada. You?"

"Ben's coworkers have a barbecue every Friday night and I wondered if you'd like to go. You can meet him and his friends."

"Sure."

"I also take sandwiches to Ben's work on Wednesdays. Want to come with me?"

"Anything to prevent death by boredom. I don't like to be cooped up inside the house."

"I'll come get you tomorrow after I make up the sandwiches."

"Hey, I can make a one-handed-sandwich. Come get me before you make them. I'll stand there and nibble while you work."

They shared a laugh. "I have a feeling you'll try to help." She eyed Mandy's hand. "But it's settled. See you tomorrow morning."

Chapter Thirteen

Wednesday after taking Reece to school and making two trays of sandwiches, Mandy rode with Amelia to a rural area on the edge of town.

The brick-fronted pole-barn building said Refuge DZ.

DZ? That was a skydiving acronym for the drop zone where people land. Pararescuers were skydivers…

A sense of impending doom settled around her.

What kind of work did Ben do? Especially at a skydiving facility that sat on the outposts of an unmapped military base?

Surely not…

Mandy grabbed the vegetable tray with her good hand. She followed Amelia, carrying a tray piled high with ham, turkey and roast beef sandwiches into the Refuge Drop Zone facility.

"Hey guys. Lunch is here." Amelia set the tray on a table in a lounge area just inside the modern facility's doors.

An Asian gentleman walked over and kissed Amelia's cheek. "Hey, sweetie." Turning to smile at Mandy, he extended his hand. "I'm Ben, Amelia's fiancé."

"Nice to meet you. I'm Mandy Manchester." Her heart pounded when someone in a PJ uniform walked behind the counter. A Hispanic man with a slight limp and who was built like a tank.

"Manchester…" Ben's eyes flashed recognition and his fingers snapped in the air. "Ah, wow. I know who you are. Nolan talks about you constantly."

Mandy's heart paused, then sputtered back into rhythm.

A door opened. The room hushed to Antarctic quiet. All eyes peered past Mandy, then to her, then past. Mandy turned.

Nolan stood in a doorway, staring at her with a semi-shocked expression.

It slowly hit Mandy where she'd seen Ben before. On the bridge the day of the collapse. Only she hadn't known his name. And he'd been dropped later, much later than the other guys. In fact, after most of the children had been rescued. He'd personally carried Reece from the bridge to the basket to the helicopter to the ambulance. He'd been dressed just like Nolan. Two and two rushed together…

Nolan and Ben were pararescue teammates. Reece was Ben's soon-to-be-stepdaughter.

Nolan eyed her, then Amelia, then the sandwiches. "I see you met Amelia."

Frozen arms growing numb, Mandy's heart sank. She faced Amelia. "You know Nolan?"

"Yeah. He works with Ben." Amelia licked her lips and looked confused for a second while understanding vied for purchase.

"So, Ben is part of the PJ team?" Mandy hated that her voice quivered.

Amelia nodded. "Yeah. You know about PJs?"

"I know some."

Amelia set down the tray and moved close. "I didn't know. Otherwise I would have told you Ben was one. With them being Special Operatives in the military, I don't really like to mention it. Not that I don't trust you. I would have eventually told you—"

"It's okay. I understand."

"You sure?"

Mind spinning to reconcile all this, Mandy merely nodded politely to help pop some of the expanding tension in the room.

"Nice to see you again," Nolan said in their general direction, then walked off.

As uncomfortable as Nolan looked right now, Mandy wasn't sure she should stay. He looked dejected, like he'd just lost his best friend.

"Obviously you two know each other. And things are noticeably tense. Is staying going to be a problem?" Amelia whispered.

"I don't know. We sort of have a history. And I sort of ordered him to stay away from me. And here I am on his turf."

Amelia encased Mandy's forearm with a gentle grip and moved in close. "I'm so sorry. I didn't realize—"

"No way you could have known. I should have mentioned Nolan to you. And would have eventually—" Mandy's mouth trembled.

A look of concern etched Amelia's features. "Let me know when you're ready. We can leave any time," she whispered.

"Okay." But she couldn't run from this. Not after she'd ordered him out of her life and then entered his domain. She needed to clear that much up at least. "Let me go talk to him a minute. Then we can leave."

Mandy gathered courage to walk over to where he sat at a table in the DZ lounge area. Nolan's back faced her. The men around him eyed her approach with mixed expressions. Some amused interest. Others more guarded and some she couldn't read if she tried. She hadn't known the meaning of intimidation until this moment. Nolan must have sensed her approach because he stilled and everyone's voices quieted.

"Excuse me. I don't mean to interrupt," Mandy said to the men around the table. "Nolan, may I please have a word with you?"

Slowly, Nolan pivoted to face her with a wary expression. Two other PJs eyed her with open, expectant gleams. Nolan narrowed his gaze at them as he rose and turned to meet her approach.

"I've got a few minutes." He waved her over to a table by the corner. Far away from everyone.

"Nolan, I didn't know you were going to be here."

He shrugged. "No problem. That all?" He leaned a tense hand on the table and eyed his watch.

She suddenly felt dismissed. Her courage diminished. A lump of emotion formed. He was acting as cold as she had to him the last time they'd talked. Maybe it was a defensive response to her reaction. He'd hardly make eye contact with her.

Tension stretched between them as her mind scrambled for the next thing to say. She drew a breath. "Anyway, I should get going so you can get back to work. I—I'm sorry if I made you uncomfortable," she said softly.

He appeared to stare behind her and shrugged his shoulders. Tense muscles still worked his jaw and cheek.

She turned and could have sworn she felt him take an instant step toward her. But he stopped when she looked over her shoulder. He shaded his expression instantly but not fast enough for her to miss the change.

Tortured was the word she'd use to describe the fleeting look in his eyes.

The irony was, he looked exactly how she felt inside.

Heart in her throat, Mandy went to Amelia, who was talking quietly with Ben, whose eyes held sympathy. "Ready?"

"Sure. See you all this weekend," Amelia said as if sensing Mandy needed to get out of here before she broke down.

Once in the car, she barely got her door shut when sobs racked her body.

Amelia backed out with one hand on the wheel and one hand on Mandy's shoulder. Her whispers told Mandy she murmured prayers.

A couple blocks away, out of sight of the DZ, Amelia pulled the car over in a vacant lot. "I'm so sorry I didn't tell you where we were going before. Maybe we could have figured out they were on the same team and avoided all this for you."

Mandy wiped her eyes with tissues she'd had to start carrying these days. "It's not your fault. You couldn't have known. And to be fair, I should have told you about Nolan sooner. I—I don't know why I didn't. I guess I thought if I didn't talk about him, the feelings would fade. Only they haven't."

"I'll understand if you don't want to go to the barbecue this weekend. It's at Joel's, their team leader. Nolan will probably be there."

"I'll have to think about it." Amelia would be disappointed if she didn't go, and frankly, she'd looked forward to going and meeting some of Amelia's friends.

She just hadn't known that Nolan would be among them.

"I don't want to make him feel uncomfortable either. I—I mean if I go."

Amelia put her hand on Mandy's arm. "You still love him. Don't you?"

"I do not. At least I don't think so. Parting was hard and I think I'm just shell-shocked by the whole thing in general."

"You mean the bridge collapse?"

"That, and seeing him again after all these years of no contact."

"If you need to talk about it, I'm here."

"I think what I need is to get a grip on my emotions."

"I think you need to get a grip on the fact that you're far from over him."

"Well, good friends will give it to you straight."

They laughed. Then Amelia grew serious. "If you're the high school sweetheart the guys tease him about, then you still hold a huge place in his heart."

"He acts like it. But that doesn't make sense. Otherwise he would have tried to find me."

That he hadn't didn't speak well of his so-called love.

"From what I gather, he did try." Amelia bit her lip and her cheeks flushed. Like she wondered how much she should say and fretted if she'd already revealed too much.

"I'd almost rather believe he didn't. Because the alternative is too painful to ponder."

If he had tried to write, someone with access to her mail obviously intercepted. The only person with that kind of access would have been Mandy's mother. And the only person who could possibly hurt her worse than Nolan by doling out that kind of betrayal would be her mom.

A thought thunderstruck her. She turned to Amelia. "He…he didn't…please tell me…he didn't put you up to this, right?"

"What?" Amelia blinked.

"Befriending me."

Amelia's nose scrunched. "Who, Nolan?"

"Yes."

Her confused expression sobered into one of sincerity. "No. I didn't even know you two knew one another, much less had a past. I befriended you because I wanted to."

"That's a relief."

"Why would you think he'd do something like that?"

"Because he would. He always thought he knew what was best for me. And so he always made my decisions for me."

"Like deciding you'd be better off broken up."

"Yes. Like that. And I just don't know if I can ever get past it. Especially when he still shows signs of having that tendency."

Amelia shifted in her seat. "Making decisions for people?"

"Yes." Mandy rolled down her window.

Amelia cut the radio. "I'll admit, Nolan is a natural problem solver."

"But what if he was wrong back then?"

"From what I gathered, he didn't share your faith. To me, that sounds like he was being more selfless than selfish."

"I hadn't thought of it that way. Seriously, I don't know if I can go through something like that again."

"That's what most people think on the front end of potential pain. But on the other side of it they realize that, with God, people can get through a lot of hard things they never thought they could. I mean, isn't Nolan worth the shot?"

Silence let her seriously ponder that.

"Yes. I believe he is. But, there are other factors now. His place on the pararescue team is in trouble and I don't even know if romance could be on his radar without compromising his placement here. Besides, I'm a basket case right now and up to my eyeballs in med school."

"No chance you guys could ever get back together? Permanently I mean?"

"I don't see how. We're facing the same dilemma as last time, only on a larger scale with both of us having more to lose."

"How so?" Amelia restarted the car and kicked on the air.

"With me having signed a three-year contract with the hospital, and him facing the possibility of being deployed somewhere on the other side of the world. We'd never see each other. Our careers seem destined to always push us apart."

"Maybe God could turn one of you around. That would pull you together."

"I don't see how. Because that would mean one of us giving up our life's dream. How would we choose? Which would be worse? Children who won't get a doctor and a community that will lack a free clinic that I've always dreamed of starting? Or those in need of rescue, going without?"

"You guys could find a way."

"Not when Nolan's future is in the hands of the military."

"Not exactly." Amelia pulled back out onto the road.

Mandy studied her.

"They're in the hands of something more powerful than even the superior United States Military."

"What's that?"

"God's hands."

"I still don't see how it's ever going to work out unless one of us gives up our dream. I'm not sure that for either of us our lifelong dreams are worth more than the other person. We've made collateral commitments that can't be broken without a lot of people being majorly hurt."

"So, what are you gonna do?"

"Keep as emotionally distant as possible. It's the only thing I know to do."

Though Amelia didn't comment, the grim doubt swiping the smile from her face said it all. One, it was going to be easier said than done. Two, Amelia's expression displayed doubt as to whether that was the best way to handle this.

"Now I've done it."

Amelia eyed her before returning her attention to the road.

"I thought as long as I steered clear of him, I'd be fine."

The problem was, now that she'd befriended Amelia, and Amelia's fiancé and Nolan were teammates and good friends, it would be next to impossible to avoid him. Amelia's friendship had become too dear to lose. So she would just have to buckle down and be strong. Face this head on. Hopefully the old feelings would once again fade after the newness of seeing him wore off.

"I just need to get through the meantime until my heart is finally free of him."

"What if it never is?"

Mandy had no answer for that.

"You've got to be kidding—" Amelia let off the gas and tapped her brakes about the time Mandy noticed the patrol car with lights and sirens whipping up on Amelia's bumper.

"I don't think I was speeding." Amelia pulled over. The police car followed suit.

Mandy eyed the speedometer. "Me, either." Maybe she disobeyed a traffic sign because Mandy distracted her or something—

"Wait…" Amelia leaned forward, viewing her side mirror. Her head whipped around and she clutched Mandy's good arm. "That's Nolan!" she squealed. "He came after you."

Mandy grunted. "In a cop car?"

That moment Nolan jogged to the window and rapped on Amelia's side. She rolled it down. Nolan seemed out of breath and he avoided Mandy's gaze a moment as he sent an imploring look to Amelia. "Mind if I borrow your seat a sec?"

Amelia eyed Mandy inquisitively.

Hands pressed on the outside of Amelia's door, he leaned in and captured Mandy's gaze with one of humility and care. "If it's all right, I'd like to borrow your best friend a minute, too."

Everything in Mandy wilted at his smile. And gorgeous eyes. Forget it. She was a goner.

Mandy nodded, feeling her pulse do triple time. What on earth was Nolan up to?

Grin plastered, Amelia rose. Nolan lowered himself into Amelia's seat. Amelia strode back to the police car and chatted with…

"Is that Officer Stallings?"

Nolan grinned and shrugged.

The irony made Mandy laugh.

"A desperate man will humble himself however he has to. Besides, Stallings owes me. I'm giving him free skydiving lessons. In fact, he pulled up for one right after you and Amelia left. So I called in a favor." His grin stretched.

She shook her head, but giddiness welled.

Nolan shifted in the seat to face her, his luscious mouth curving. "What?"

"I can't believe you had us pulled over just to talk to me."

He reached for her hand. "Mandy, I…" He swallowed. "I don't even know what to say except that I don't want things to be this way between us." He drew a breath and held her gaze. "Like, back there at the DZ. And not seeing you for weeks." He shook his head.

She squeezed his hand which melted warmth up her arm. "I know."

He brushed hair from her forehead. "I can do a lot of hard things, but sitting in the same room with you and not talking isn't one of them."

"It's tough for me, too, Nolan." Her voice felt raw.

"I never, ever meant to hurt you. So please, Mandy, I am begging you to get help."

She recoiled from his hand. Pain streamed back in.

This wasn't about rekindling them and him finally trusting that she could make sound choices. This was, as usual, about him fixing her. Granted, she might need the counseling and would consider it. After all, she couldn't help others if she wasn't healthy. Still, Nolan's words stung. She'd hoped he wanted to be with her for love and not pity.

"I don't need you to rescue me, Nolan."

"That's not what this is about."

He glared. She glared. A war of wills stood in the space between them.

She jabbed her finger toward the ditch side of the road. "Out. I will not discuss this further." Because if she did, she'd lose control and he'd know how very much he still meant to her.

Remorse and confusion flickered in his face.

"Please, Nolan. Go." She dipped her chin before he could read her face and dig to the deeper issue.

Chapter Fourteen

"**Y**ou okay?" Amelia asked when Nolan was gone and they were back on the road.

Mandy shrugged.

"I'll understand if you don't want to go."

Mandy knew Amelia referred to the invitation to a weekend barbecue at her fiancé's coworker's home.

"And you should probably know that Nolan is almost always there, too." Amelia's voice had quieted the more she spoke.

"It's all right. I can still go. I want to spend time with you. I needed this friendship as much as I suspect you did." And truth be known, she wanted to see Nolan again.

Amelia adjusted her hair clip. "Don't get me wrong, Celia and Amber are two of my closest friends. But they have a bond that no one can penetrate. I've been praying for a best friend like that. A friendship like what they have."

"You're an answer to my prayers for a best friend, too, Amelia." Mandy hugged her. "Ugh. I'm never this sappy. I don't know…since the bridge collapse, where I literally saw people die right in front of me, I guess I've seen how important it is to tell people how I feel. How much they mean to me."

"What about Nolan?"

"Wow. The Bible's right. Faithful are the wounds of a friend. You don't pull any punches, do you?"

"No. And you didn't answer my question. So let me answer it for you. Life is too short not to love until it hurts."

"But love hurts."

"But life hurts worse without love. And life is too short not to let those you love know it. And love is too precious not to let those who've hurt you have a chance to make it right."

"I get what you're saying. I don't want to open things up that will turn me into an emotional train wreck."

Amelia snickered. "Honey, that engine already ran off the track. You are a wreck...*right now*, but a wreck is not *who you are*."

Mandy fingered the lace seam on her layered shirt hem.

"Let God fill that broken place, Mandy. Because even then, you tried to fill it with Nolan. And as great as he is, he can't be everything for you."

A mental lightbulb clicked on. She looked at Amelia, shocked that her young friend would come to the conclusion Mandy should have years ago. "But I depended on him to be."

"Only God can be everything we need. The minute we start depending on our husbands to be everything we need, our relationship gets as shaky as a washing machine out of balance."

"But he's not my husband."

"Yet."

"I don't know what you mean."

Amelia patted her on the knee in a pretend-patronizing manner. "All right Miss Med School Valedictorian, you're way too smart to play so dumb. Friendship Rule Number One. Never ever fib to your best friend."

Mandy laughed.

"He is the man you love." Amelia hiked a thumb toward her back window where the police cruiser had sat. "I just saw it in your eyes and in his and I sensed it when I prayed in my mind while chatting it up with Stallings. And I suspect if you were praying, you would, too. You two are destined to be together."

Mandy climbed the steps to Ivy Manor Thursday evening, looking forward to crawling into bed. Exhaustion clung to her after an all-day shopping trip in St. Louis with Amelia for wedding stuff. Mandy smiled. They'd had a blast. Now Mandy needed to go in and call her mom, who was recovering from chemo.

Down the hall, a shadow in front of her door shifted and stood. She froze, prepared to scuttle back out the door.

"It's me, Mandy. Hall light's burned out. Be careful." Nolan flipped on a pen light to direct her path. "I told the maintenance man, but he hasn't returned to repair it yet. I'd do it myself except I don't have the equipment with me." Annoyance tinged his voice as he aimed a penlight at his watch.

"What are you doing here?" She stepped closer.

He looked for a moment like he might try to reach for her but he stuffed his hands in his pockets. "I gave you up once, Mandy. Don't make me do it again."

She blinked furiously to try to see through the darkness. "Nolan, you confuse the daylights out of me. One minute I think you're just hanging around because you feel sorry for me. The next minute it seems like you still—" Her mouth clamped shut.

Moving close, he grasped her hand and elbow. "Still what, Mandy?"

"Like you still might possibly love me." She'd whispered it so low, didn't know if he'd heard.

He dropped his chin to his chest and chuckled. Chuckled!

Before she could stomp his toes to bone dust, he pulled her into sheltering arms. "Might possibly, Mandy?"

The gently mocking question froze her.

"Forgive me for being so vague then." His voice dropped

deep and grungy. Before she could diagnose what was happening, his mouth closed over hers in a soldier-sure kiss that turned her knees to noodles.

Her brain reduced to mush, she applied herself to the experience that was nothing like the clumsy kiss on a long-ago jungle gym.

His lips were as warm as the intense compassion always flaring in his deeply enchanting eyes.

She leaned into the strength of his tightening embrace and let the care and emotion of it take her away. His lips lingered over hers for another mesmerizing moment. A vulnerably revealing kiss that left no doubt that he loved her with his whole entire being.

Then he made the excruciating break and tugged her to his chest. He was squashing her injured arm, but hey, who was complaining?

"I'm concerned about the trauma you've endured, Mandy, and how it's affecting you and the future that I hope to have with you." He bent his head and kissed the top of hers, looking very much like he wanted to kiss her mouth again instead.

Obnoxious light flooded the hallway.

She groaned. "Guess the maintenance man made it back."

"Apparently." He slipped his arms from around her waist and tucked his thumb in his jeans. "I should let you get some sleep."

Sleep? Just why did a person need it? Why couldn't life consist of daylight and Nolan's kisses?

He reached in her purse and scrounged for her keys. A confused look crossed his face. "No way!" he said in one word and dug like her dog did in the dirt under Ivy Manor's fence when going after the yard gofer that taunted him.

But Nolan couldn't produce the keys.

Mandy started giggling. He shot her a mock ire grin.

She smothered a snort when in a flash of digging in apparent panic that he'd lost his magical touch, he still couldn't find them. War alight in his eyes, he knelt and turned her purse upside down and dumped the contents out on the hallway floor.

She gasped a yelp and covered her mouth but guffaws still slipped past as he dropped to his hands and knees. Frantic fingers scattered the materials across the carpet until a flash of silver met the steel blue determination in his eyes.

"There they are." He jerked them above his head in a motion of victory.

"That's the first time you've not found them on the first try." Another giggle escaped. The lights flickered.

"Ha-ha. Go ahead and gloat, being you're the reason my coordination is off. That kiss was—wowza." He scooped her stuff back into her purse while she broke out in blushes.

She rose with him. "Wowza?"

"Wow-wow-wowza." He leaned in, looking intent on another one.

The hall lights buzzed, then shut off again.

Much as she longed for the emotional reconnection wrought by the last kiss, this hallway was way too dark and intimate. And his kisses way too potent and his grin too virile. It would be way too easy for her to ask him in. Then *wowza* could turn to *whoops.* Not so much her body but her heart.

She ducked inside her door before both their resolves crumbled. "Goodbye, Nolan."

His hand pressed his chest and he gave a mock-fatal slump. "Ah. Woman, you wound me. I hate the sound of goodbye. Can't you say, 'See you tomorrow, Nolan' instead?" All joking aside, a vulnerable query entered his eyes.

"You going to the barbecue at Joel's on Friday?"

An intoxicating grin breaking forth like the beautiful southern Illinois sunrises she'd come to look forward to and love, he leaned against the wall, and nodded.

"Then, I'll see you tomorrow, Nolan."

Chapter Fifteen

"I slept better last night than I have in weeks," Mandy said to Nolan the next evening, after she and he, Amelia and Ben arrived early at the barbecue.

"You had a long nap in the car today, too." He shuffled his hand across her head. They'd just returned from a six-hour drive to central Illinois and back with Ben and Amelia. They took Hutton, Ben's special needs brother, halfway to Chicago where his mom met them.

"I enjoyed meeting Amelia's future mother-in-law. I didn't realize Ben and Hutton's father recently passed away."

"Yeah. Major heart attack. Ben and Hutton took it pretty hard, as did their mom. Hutton's going back to live with her so Ben and Amelia can finalize wedding plans."

"Hutton seems pretty advanced for someone with Down syndrome."

"He has Mosaic. Not as limiting as regular Down, which you probably know."

As was the custom at the Friday night barbecues, the evening's early birds walked along the leaf-carpet trail in the woods behind Joel's house while waiting for the others to arrive.

Foot crunches sounded behind them. "Yo, dudes. Cut thrust," Vince called.

Mandy turned with Nolan, who slowed to let Vince, a ways down the trail, catch up.

Ben and Amelia, walking hand in hand in front of Nolan and Mandy, paused.

"Uh, why's he carrying an axe?" Mandy eyed Vince jogging toward them.

"We bring back firewood for roasting marshmallows later."

"Ah. So, cut thrust means…?"

Nolan grinned. "Wait up."

She nodded. "Got it."

"In case you haven't figured it out yet, this is sort of a tradition." Nolan bumped her shoulder as they walked, longing to hold her hand like Ben did Amelia's and, further up the trail, Joel did Amber's. Celia and Manny hadn't arrived yet.

"The barbecue?"

"All of it. This woodsy walk. Eating together. Then we gather around a campfire, tell stories and roast marshmallows."

"And make s'mores?" Her face lit up like the lightning bugs hovering at the edge of the trees lining both sides of the rustic, woodsy trail.

"Yeah, s'mores. Then Ben whips out his guitar and plays." Nolan cleared his throat. Should he mention to Mandy that Ben usually played his original worship songs later in the night?

"Sounds like fun. I'm glad I came." This time, she pressed her shoulder into his, and sent him a toothpaste-commercial-grade smile. "And that we cleared the air."

"Me, too." He clasped her hand. A thrill went through him when she didn't stiffen or let go.

Beside him, Vince waggled his eyebrows. He dramatically slowed his pace and looked Mandy up and down, then gave Nolan a thumbs-up sign.

Nolan shot him a caustic look.

Vince smirked and jogged ahead.

Farther down the trail, they slowed as they approached Chance, crouched down at the edge of a stand of trees. His shoulders and head were thrust between a bungle of bushes hedging a fenced-in field.

He peeked up at their approach. "Check this out," he whispered and waved them over.

Nolan directed Mandy beside him. She knelt to his left and Vince to his right.

A group of squirrels squirmed in a lustrous gray, white and brown spinning pile. Furry heads and fluffy tails bobbed and dipped in and out of the middle. Something brown lay shredded at their feet.

"What are they doing?" Mandy asked.

"Ravaging through a peanut sack Chance tossed over there," Nolan answered in low tones. "Chance here is our resident animal freak. He has a way with wildlife that is miraculous to watch."

She blinked big doe eyes at him. "Miraculous. Another Christian-y word."

"That's my cue. I'm outta here," Vince said. He stood and moved closer to Chance, feet away.

Mandy shifted closer to Nolan. "Speaking of miracles, I never would have dreamed of hearing that word come out of your mouth when you were younger." She watched him a moment longer, a look of awe filling her face. "Look, I even have goose bumps breaking out." She raised her good arm.

Goosebumps prickled up over his scalp right now, too.

At that moment, he shifted to face her and their gazes locked. The space between them telescoped. A connection synced back and forth and neither could motivate themselves to look away. Nolan issued a kind smile. That and his nearness must have proved too much. She tilted away and returned her attention to the squirrels.

"How bittersweet that you are walking with the Lord now and I'm not," she whispered. Pain streaked across her face.

How badly she missed Him. Both of them. God, and Nolan. Mandy scrunched her burning eyelids shut before traitorous moisture gave her away. Not fast enough. A solitary tear slipped through.

Nolan lifted a finger to brush along her cheek. Scared of her own reaction, she started to angle her face away but noticed the other PJs intently watching. For whatever reason, she let Nolan wipe her tear. Something in her didn't want to compromise his reputation with these brave men who respected and loved him. Nor impose negativity on the bulletproof bond this fiercely protective, rescuing band of brothers had.

The urge to explain herself and her feeble emotions overtook her. Just as she opened her mouth to form an excuse for her tears, the men politely turned away and began watching the squirrels once more.

Mandy settled in the keenly comfortable presence of these titanium-tough but acutely sensitive warriors, and trained her attention on the fuzzy rodents that Chance found so interesting.

Delight skittered through her within seconds of watching them scurry about. The large gray squirrel sat back on its haunches and held a nut between its paws. Teeth nibbled as claws worked the peanut around and around.

"Ready?" Nolan stood and reached a hand down for her. Mandy eyed the other two PJs who stayed crouched. This meant the invitation was for her only.

She took his hand and let him pull her up from the embankment. The last thing she needed was to fall and further damage her already broken wrist on the uneven terrain.

Once back at Joel's property after the hike, Mandy rubbed a hand along her sweaty forehead. "I'm glad for a thing called deodorant."

Nolan chuckled, but sniffed long and elephant-snout-loud.

Self-consciousness she wasn't accustomed to jolted through her at the thought of reeking like sweat in front of him.

"You only smell like honeysuckle." Mirth peppered his words.

"Fibber." She gave his arm a gentle sock.

"Want something to drink?" Mandy asked as they approached a cooler. She tried to open it with one hand. Wouldn't work. Frustration gritted her teeth. She needed two hands to—

Nolan's hand joined hers to undo the latch. Goose bumps came to her arms at the gentle, innocent contact.

Or maybe not so innocent. Seemed to her that for a man who could scale cloud-altitude glaciers and fly parachutes with an M-16 on his back in the blindfolds of darkness toward terrorist-riddled terrain, it was taking Nolan longer to open the scuffed up cooler than it ought. Her suspicions confirmed when his hand brushed hers.

Strong fingers flexed and the latch gave way, but his arm stayed. Forearm muscles bunched, he angled his chin down toward his shoulder, now melded against hers. Body in a gentle sway, he studied her face like one testing tepid waters. His eyes turned a persuasive shade of blue. His breath feathered her face and his skin warmed hers. Nerve endings awakened and brought to life longing for the delightful contact to continue. Her consuming want for closeness and the kiss he seemed suddenly intent on caused her mind to clear from the brilliant fog. She tensed. And disengaged.

But as nothing else had escaped his radar attention today, he watched her carefully enough to signal her that he noticed.

A disarming grin made her knees go as soft as ultrasound gel and her mind as hazy as the screen. He passed her a soft drink that she would have chosen for herself.

When had he even opened the cooler lid?

"Frightening how well you still know me," she managed when words finally returned to her.

"Yeah." His voice held a strange thickness.

Soda set down, he pushed a tendril of hair off her forehead and tucked it behind her ear. "I—"

Just then his gaze lifted to a view past her shoulders. Head lifting, his visual trajectory tracked across the yard. An odd and increasingly comical expression coated his face as he looked past her—and laughed.

A morbidly obese cat darted across the lush green yard with something peculiar attached to its—

Mandy leaned in. "Does that cat have a bandage on its butt?"

"Yeah. Got speared in the rump by a robin. Got too close to its eggs, I guess."

Their laughter conjoined as they watched the cat frolic.

"Name's Psychoticat. Psych for short." Nolan popped the top on her soda.

"Interesting." She sipped and languished in Nolan's laughter and the feel of carbonation as sweet soda made its way down.

"He's pretty cool, actually. Used to belong to Amber but when she and Joel adopted Bradley, the cat had to go. Bradley's allergic and has asthma."

"Who has him now?"

"Celia and Manny. Celia tries to act like she hates the cat, but snuggles with him when she thinks no one's looking. Psych has an imported marble water dish and a throne for a bed."

"She spoils the cat?"

"Yeah, but when she knows someone's coming over, she shoves all the evidence in the front coat closet. The one she keeps empty for such an occasion."

"Hey, most women have a place to shove and stuff things like baskets of dirty clothes when unexpected company arrives."

"Where's your place?"

"In my shower."

Chuckles came from Nolan as he gestured toward the food

table. Her stomach growled as she reached for a plate. He intercepted her. "Point out what you want. I'll fix yours, then mine."

She went around both sides of a long table, covered with serving platters full of delectable-smelling food. "I think I'll take one of everything."

Nolan's grin was sweeter than anything on the table. "And with your still-trim figure, where do you propose putting it?"

Propose.

The word ripped the smile from her face and put a raw place in her throat. Her appetite started receding, but the smell of Celia's famed enchilada pie won the battle.

After setting her plate down, he fixed his own plate with the others. The PJs and their family and friends made it back to the tables. Everyone took places around her, except they left vacant the space next to her.

Nolan returned and lifted his leg over the bench, lowering himself beside her. Naturally, as if this was his place.

Plunging her fork awkwardly into the enchilada pie, Mandy lifted it to her mouth. The red and orange and brown juicy concoction fell back onto her plate. After another failed attempt, Nolan extracted the fork from her hand.

He fed her a bite, then dabbed her mouth with a napkin. When his gaze rested on her lips then skimmed up to her eyes, his expression changed. Then he tensed his jaw and looked away.

She wished he didn't. Then wished she didn't.

Her hand snaked out and reached for a carrot stick. She jabbed it a tad too hard into the ranch dressing. She enjoyed the feel of the cool, fibrous carrot in her finger and loved the crunch as she bit into it.

"You're still a texture junkie, aren't you?" He displayed a smile that brought out the intricate kindness of his face.

She thought about it a minute. "Yeah. I guess I am."

"Thought so. I always thought that so unique about you.

How you would stop and feel the texture of everything and languish in it. Flowers, material, surfaces of any sort." His voice trailed off and something bitter flashed in his eyes, making her think the memories suddenly pained him. He looked at his own food and swallowed before he'd ever even taken a bite.

They ate in semi-comfortable silence as she and Nolan tuned in and contributed to the other conversations around them. Room was tight and a couple times when he shifted to listen to Brock, on the other side of him, his broad shoulder and part of his back brushed up against hers. Much to the protest of her mind, warmth and longing claimed her every time it happened.

Vince and Chance approached. "Where's Mooch?"

Mandy wiped her mouth. "He's at home."

"You're welcome to bring him," Celia said.

"We'll go get him if you'll give us your apartment keys."

Mandy stood and pulled them from her jeans pocket.

"Speaking of Mooch, I wonder what all he has torn up," she asked moments after the guys left to get him and Nolan returned with the dessert she'd pointed out.

Nolan laughed. "Probably the couch. Least he can't tear up your non-existent coffee tables."

She set down her fork. Glad to be able to feed herself the dessert at least, because it stuck to the utensil. As did her tongue to the roof of her mouth when she tried to form an excuse for her shoddy furnishings. She could call it shabby-chic but that'd be a lie.

His arm nudged hers. "Hey, that wasn't a slam. I admire you for how hard you've worked and all you've sacrificed to get where you are."

All she'd sacrificed?

He had no idea. No idea that his statement encompassed them. What they'd had. And to be truthful, sitting here with him wrought wonder about all she'd missed over the years. Watching him mature into the magnificent man he'd become.

What she'd miss from now on if she let him slip away a second time.

She'd miss knowing the joy of only-Nolan wit and the blessing of wise, unpretentious advice. Hearing his spontaneous laughter. Seeing the loving looks and knowing she was the sole recipient. The honor of witnessing humor frolic like an adorable child in his eyes.

What would his children be like? What would it be like to mother them? What would it be like to marry this man and know that they'd never have to say goodbye again? To live out the rest of her days watching his beautiful faith grow? To dance in his arms and melt in his magnetic kisses? What would it be like to—

"It's good. You should try it."

She jerked. "What?"

Nolan motioned at the forkful of banana bar suspended in front of Mandy's mouth.

Jolted from her musings, heat rushed Mandy's cheeks and an unexpected laugh squeaked out. "You mean rather than sit here and stare at it?" She tasted a bite. "Oh. My. Stars. I want this recipe."

And I want my life back with Nolan. For good.

"Amelia made them. She can give you the recipe," Nolan offered.

Powerful longing that had nothing to do with banana bars pricked Mandy as she watched Amelia and Ben, stationed snug like lovebirds across from her and Nolan.

"Sure. Just remind me later." Amelia turned to wash Reece's face.

Mandy plowed into the cake-like moisture and rolled cream cheese icing across her tongue. But her mind wasn't on the morsel. It mulled a question she hadn't entertained since entering residency.

Had parting with Nolan been worth it?

And would parting with him again be worth the deep, black excavated void that would hollow her life without him?

Chapter Sixteen

"What kind of doctor will you be?" Amber, Joel's wife, sat beside Mandy at the picnic table at next week's barbecue. Seemed to Mandy they'd been making a concerted effort to get to know her. They'd made her feel incredibly welcome the first week.

"A pediatrician."

"She's wanted that since she was five-years-old," a deep voice said above her shoulder.

Nolan.

Her heart beat a frenzied rhythm beneath her sternum as she turned and met his smile.

"So when do you get that cast off?" Joel asked after everyone went through the food line and settled onto chairs or benches.

"Next week. And I get to return to work, too."

Now seated beside her, Nolan stopped slathering mustard on his hamburger bun and leaned in. "Say what?"

She dabbed her mouth with a napkin. "I've been cleared to go back next week."

Plate down, Nolan tapped her elbow and gave a discreet backward nod toward a weeping willow tree on the other side of Joel's yard. He rose and she followed, feeling doomed.

"Who cleared you?" Nolan asked under the tree.

She'd never seen a more steely gaze.

"My hand surgeon."

"Riviera know?"

"Since he did the surgery, yes. He was an orthopedic surgeon prior to becoming an oncologist."

"I meant does he know you're still having such difficulty sleeping and concentrating?"

"I've been better."

"You're putting your patients' lives at risk. You have every sign of PTSD." This wasn't Nolan talking. This was an elite United States airman who refused to fail or back down from a fight he knew needed winning or from a mission in need of mastering.

Her shoulders slumped. Tremors claimed her legs and a headache vaporized from nowhere. She fought for control of her voice. "Fine. I concede. You're right, Nolan. Exactly right. But by the same token, I have to get my clinic hours in."

He looked startled a moment, like he hadn't expected her to give in so easily. Walking over to her, he knelt on one knee in front of her. Suddenly her heart sped up. She willed it to stop.

Good thing because he merely pulled her down on the garden bench beside him.

His hand rested on her shoulder. "Look, I know how hard this is for you. I know how bad you've wanted this all your life. But, please, don't go back to work until you've had a psych consult. You're not ready."

After four consecutive sets of knocking, Nolan sped down Ivy Manor's hall and tapped lightly on the landlady's door. Fear tried to pound a hole through his chest using his fisted heart as a weapon. Impatience mounted until he caught sounds of the elderly woman shuffling to the door.

"It's me, Miss Ivy."

Rattling sounded as she unhooked the chain and cracked open the door. When recognition dawned, the door swung all the way. "Well, hello there, Nolan. How are you?"

He raked a hand across the back of his neck. "I'd be better if I knew Mandy was okay."

Concern puckered her face. "Oh?"

"She returned to light duty this week but didn't show up for her shift today."

Lines deepened in her face. "Let me grab my robe." Moments later she joined him in the hall. Keys jangled as she pulled one out from the middle and poked it into Mandy's keyhole.

She started to move inside, but when the dog rushed the door instead of Mandy, Nolan halted her. "Miss Ivy, let me go in first. In fact, I'd prefer you wait out here."

If, God forbid, something bad happened, Miss Ivy didn't need to find her. Images and fear shoved his legs to longer, swifter strides across Mandy's eerily quiet living room.

Adrenaline quivered fingers that pushed open her bedroom door. Alarm rushed through him at the sound of a box fan she kept by her bed and only used while she slept.

"Mandy." He stepped in, eyes adjusting to darkness.

A still lump on the bed put a stiff lump in his throat. Panic rose. Instantly at her side, he brushed blankets aside. "M-Mandy?" Relief swarmed him when her chest rose and fell and her skin emitted warmth onto his slick palms. He knelt on the floor beside the bed. "Mandy?" He pressed his hand into her shoulder.

Dull and vacant eyes opened slowly. She murmured something unintelligible and blinked several times at him. Then warbled up and snatched up the clock. "Oh! I'm so late!" Comforter flung aside, she stood but wobbled.

His hands circled her. "Dr. Riviera told me he had to prescribe different sleeping pills this week. How many did you take?" He flicked on the light and assessed her pupils.

"I—only two. Four hours apart like you're supposed to."

Hand at her throat, she slid from his grasp and scrambled around for shoes that were directly in front of her. "Can't believe this. I've never been late—"

Rattled as she looked, she had no business working today. Especially not when her work entailed putting people's lives in her quaking hands.

"Mandy, Riviera can replace you for your shift today."

"No, we're short. Other residents are on vacation." She sat back down. "I jeopardized my position and overslept." Groaning, she picked up her alarm clock and eyed the glaring numbers. "By two hours. I've never, ever in my life overslept. Not even a minute."

"Your body obviously needed it." Kneeling, he peeled her shoes back off, intent on making her lie back down and get more rest. He rose. "Be right back." He needed to let Miss Ivy know Mandy was all right. He left her room to do so, then returned.

"Was that Miss Ivy?"

Nolan's jaw quivered. "Yes. Riviera sent me here to check on you. She let me in."

Distraught eyes widened. "I'm so sorry, Nolan. You should be concentrating on your job. Not minding me like an irresponsible child." Frustration seethed through her voice, but Nolan didn't get the idea she was irritated with him. More herself.

His suspicions confirmed when she jerked the prescription bottle off the nightstand. Pills rattled. "Oh, Nolan, how am I to function without sleep? I can't take these. At least not at this dosage." She sighed.

"Mandy, you need professional help. These symptoms, they've gone on too long."

"Please tell me you didn't say that to Dr. Riviera."

"Not my place to."

"Oh, good—"

"Yet." He folded arms across his chest.

She tensed. "And that means?"

"If things don't improve, I will intervene."

"Nolan, you'll jeopardize my career." She wrestled her hair into a twist and secured it off her neck with a clip.

He stood and broadened his stance. "If you go to work with the amount of sleep you've been getting, you'll jeopardize lives."

"I appreciate your concern about my patients." She shoved her feet into her shoes. "You're right. I'll consider counseling."

"I'm equally concerned about you."

Her movements stuttered so that must have thrown her off. Confusion settled over her face, as though she couldn't think what she was about to say for a second. Then her face cleared and sharpened. "I won't put anyone at risk. I'll make sure he lowers my dosage. I do feel refreshed after a good night's sleep." She threw on her lab coat. "I'm fine."

"Really?" A muscle worked in his jaw.

"Really." She tried to brush past him.

Arm out like a wooden railroad barrier, he pressed her shoulder, prohibiting her passing. "Then tell me one thing, Mandy."

She strung her stethoscope around her neck. "What?"

He leaned in, putting sternness to his voice. "Why is it, if you're okay to go to work, that you have your lab coat on inside out?" His finger flicked the tag on the outside of her collar.

Nolan was right. Exactly right. But, then why couldn't she get hold of another resident to take her OB call? Mandy tried several other numbers, then jammed her phone in her purse and hiked faster to the hospital since it was blocks away and her car was still in the shop. Maybe one would be there and she could ask them to take her shift.

Her beeper went off. Refuge OB ward calling. Mandy picked up her pace and dialed back as best she could with one arm. "Yes?"

"Dr. Manchester?"

"Yes."

"This is Raven from OB. A teen patient came in, twenty-seven weeks, in labor. We've started an IV. We can't get a hold of the other resident who was going to take your call after surgery."

"Neither can I. Maybe they had complications. Regardless, I'll be there in a minute. Bolus her with fluids and follow the other preterm labor protocol." Mandy sprinted the rest of the way.

Once in the room, a nurse approached her. "She's dilating."

"Start Mag. Give her a forty-gram bolus."

The nurse's brow cinched. "You mean four?"

"Four. Yes. What did I say?" Mandy felt warmth drain from her face.

The nurse grabbed a bag of IV fluids and gave Mandy a concerned, yet disapproving stare. "Forty."

Mandy's hands trembled as she dialed the resident once more. Finally, someone answered. "Yes," her voice cracked in the middle. "I need you up here now. Please. Labor room seven. I'm in no condition to stay. Thank you."

Dr. Riviera motioned to a chair across the desk in his office the next day. "Come on in, Dr. Manchester. What's on your mind?"

She sat. "First off, I need to apologize about coming in late yesterday."

He nodded. "Understandable. Not like you've made a habit of it. In fact, I don't recall you ever being late. How's your hand faring?"

"Better. I became quite ambidextrous in the past six weeks." She cleared her throat. "But my hand isn't why I'm here."

He lowered his head and eyed her over his glasses.

"I can't return to patient care yet." Mandy's mouth trembled as she pushed the words past the memory of the near-lethal medication error she'd almost made today.

Sweat broke out behind her neck at what could have

happened had an experienced nurse not caught it, pulled her aside and called her on it. She mentally kicked herself for negating Nolan's words. Like refusing to believe it would negate the truth: she'd turned into a mental wreck.

"I was only coming in today to let you know I need time off. I got caught in a situation where a patient needed a doctor and they were all tied up. I had no choice but to give orders."

"The unit's swamped. You seem alert right now. Do you want to try to finish out the shift?"

"No." She stood. "Absolutely not." She swallowed, hoping that would help the words come easier. "I nearly gave a teenage preterm laboring patient and her baby ten times too much magnesium sulfate today."

His face paled. "Well, Mandy, were you trying to keep the girl from having a baby…or from breathing?"

She shot him a look. "It's nothing to joke about."

"Look, I know it's serious. But you caught it."

"No. I didn't. An experienced nurse did. What if she'd been too new to know?"

His mouth stretched into a grim line.

"Lack of sleep can flux your judgment."

"I rested better last night than in all the nights combined since the accident. I was fresh up on medications commonly used in labor and delivery. And I still nearly killed two people today."

His chest rose with a long breath.

"I felt scalpel sharp today once I got here. Refreshed. Not groggy. But part of being a resident means being perpetually on call. Right now, with my symptoms, I need to seek professional help. I won't be able to depend on a sleep aid being on call."

"What symptoms?" He removed his glasses and looked concerned. "Because if it's just lack of sleep, I can take you off call."

She shook her head before she lost her nerve. "Nolan Briggs voiced concern a while ago about me exhibiting signs of PTSD. I didn't listen to him at first. I thought maybe he'd just been looking too hard for symptoms since he's specializing in PTSD counseling."

"I didn't realize he was doing that." He leaned back in his chair. "Is he leaving Pararescue?"

"No. It's something he's always wanted to do. Besides rescue people. Now, he can do both."

Riviera's fingers steepled and touched his upper lip. "You do realize if I take you off duty, you won't be able to complete your residency when expected."

She swallowed. "Yes. I also realize the reason I wanted to be a doctor in the first place was to help save lives. I feel until I receive emotional help, I'm endangering lives instead."

Metal grated against wood as he opened a drawer and pulled out a card. "I'm talking as your doctor now and not your supervisor. I recommend this counseling center. It's across the street from the hospital."

She took the paper. "Thank you."

His pen clicked as he suspended it over a notepad. "Now, I'm speaking as your supervisor. I know you'll make a great physician. I normally wouldn't do this. But I'm going to propose a way for you to get clinic hours required to finish out the residency program and take your boards."

"I don't know what to say."

"Don't say anything until you hear my idea. You may not be so keen on saying yes." The corners of his eyes crinkled as he smiled. "Refuge City Council is planning a weekend benefit for victims of the bridge collapse and their families. They are asking for a hospital-affiliated employee to represent us. I think you could be that representative. Especially since you are a bridge-collapse survivor."

"And that will count toward my clinic hours?"

"Absolutely. You'd be providing a service to the community. You, along with the other benefit committee members, can brainstorm ideas on a hospital-affiliated booth."

"Safe things like handing out brochures and certificates for free health screenings?"

"Both of those sound great. See, I knew I chose the right woman for the job." He stood. "Go home. Rest. Make an appointment with the counseling center. I think you need emotional R and R as well as physical. You've been through a lot the past two months."

She nodded, but strangely, Nolan's face rather than the bridge collapse came to mind. Dr. Riviera's words tuned her back in.

"…and one catch to all this is I will not be able to allow you to return to patient care until your counselor releases you."

"Not a problem. It's safer for everyone that way."

"You don't know what hoops they're gonna want you to jump through in order to be cleared for duty. Might take longer and be tougher than you anticipate. Just be prepared for that, okay?"

She nodded, something in her gut echoing his admonition.

He's right. It's going to be tougher than you think.

Chapter Seventeen

Nolan stepped outside into the Heart of Refuge Counseling Center and set his lunch down on a vacant table.

"You should find a shady spot."

Nolan whipped around and blinked. "Mandy?"

She offered a feeble smile and plucked at a mangled sandwich.

He rose from the table, gathered his own lunch and settled across from her. "Mind if I sit with you?"

"'Course not." But her tone said differently. So she was back to being hostile again…like on the bridge.

He sat and prayed over his food.

She didn't join him. Just kept picking at her meal.

"Do you have a patient here today?" he asked.

Her eyes darkened. "Yeah, me."

Food abandoned, he reached for her hands. "Mandy, I'm sorry. What happened?"

"You should be pleased with yourself, Nolan. You were right. For a healer, I sure know how to wound." She rose.

"Wait." He surged to the other side of the table. "What are you really doing here?" He looked deep in her eyes. Or tried to.

She turned away. "Getting therapy." She chucked her

uneaten food into the trashcan and flipped a defeated look over her shoulder. "Your prediction came true. I nearly caused the death of a mother and her unborn child last week."

Nausea accosted him over not going to Riviera himself. He'd seen all the signs in Mandy. Even the other guys on the team had noticed when she'd bring lunch to the DZ with Amelia on Wednesdays, and on barbecue nights.

They'd all voiced concern.

And Nolan hadn't gone with his gut and contacted her supervisor.

He clenched his fist around his sandwich and hurled it into the trash. His appetite accompanied it.

He started after her, reaching her just inside the door. "Mandy, wait."

She paused but didn't turn around.

He curled his hand around her shoulder. "I'm sorry. I feel partly responsible."

"No, you were right, Nolan. I should have gotten help sooner. Now my career may be in ruins."

Cold shivers marched down the muscles straddling his spine as truth sank in.

They'd wound up in the same predicament. Both of their careers were jeopardized. And if they fell completely in love again, they might end up being separated. Could their love survive it a second time?

With God, yes. "Mandy, God will work this out if you trust."

She dropped her gaze. "I was resistant because I didn't want it to be true."

"But ignoring the problem won't make it go away, Mandy. You are a tough survivor who can take care of yourself and anyone else, even in the face of a horrific disaster."

"I'm trained to do that, Nolan, as are you."

"So tell me what's really going on. Or, at least tell your counselor."

Sighing, she faced him. "I don't know. I was really, really upset about not hearing from you for the first couple of years. But then I grew to understand and eventually accept the separation. It finally made sense. I thought I was fine."

"Until?"

"Until I saw you again. On the bridge. I know you did what was best for both of us in the long run. Never mind that it really, really upset me in the short run." She gave a self-deprecating laugh. "I was devastated at not hearing from you. But I thought I was over it."

He studied her hands, compulsively fiddling with her sleeves.

"I spent too many years and tears wondering why you never called, never wrote."

Speaking of compulsion—he bit his tongue from the overwhelming urge to refute that. What he had to say would only make things worse and add insult to injury.

Anger settled around her mouth. "You promised. You lied."

"I didn't—" He clenched his jaw.

Her eyes implored for truth. "Why, Nolan? Did I, our friendship, not mean enough? Did you forget? Or did you never intend to keep in touch?"

In that moment, epiphany hit. It was the not knowing why that haunted her. He scraped a hand along the back of his neck. "That's not it." His flesh needed her to understand he wasn't the villain. But this wasn't about him. What was best for her? How would she take it if she knew? "I never lied to you, Mandy."

A look of torture claimed her face. "Yes you did. I know we agreed to break up. But I didn't realize how it would break up my heart and challenge my ability to ever love again."

He'd known that hurt was a possibility. Just not the depth of it. And he hadn't known she'd never recover from it. He'd known parting would be hard. Parting had shredded his heart, too. His only consolation had been the thoughts that she'd meet someone else, fall in love and be happy and realize her dreams. That she'd get completely over him.

He'd been wrong, so wrong.

And there was no way to make it right.

Chapter Eighteen

"There is one way. Tell her the truth," Joel said later at the DZ.

Nolan rubbed hands over his eyes and forehead. "I don't want to further strain her relationship with her mom."

"God can make a way."

"How?" Nolan lifted his face to meet his team leader's gaze.

"I don't know how. Don't have to know and neither do you. Just have to trust, and commit her to Him. Commit this whole situation to Him. He's faithful, Nolan."

"I fear she's irrevocably hurt."

"I know you feel that now. But Jesus can heal her."

"Only way I feel right now is as if someone is ripping my heart through my throat."

Images of Mandy's words from before stormed through his mind.

"I hate you, Nolan. As passionately as I loved you, with everything in me, everything I had. Now it's turned to hate."

He knew better. She didn't hate him. That was just her way of coping with emotions she couldn't control right now and outcomes she couldn't control later. And she'd never say such things if she weren't suffering from PTSD.

"I realize God is giving me a second chance. I messed up the first time."

"Sure about that?" Joel watched his face like American soldiers looking to snuff out roadside bombs on Iraqi streets.

"Don't know. Maybe I made the right choice. Maybe I didn't. But I do know God has brought us back together for a reason."

Unfortunately, Mandy's bitter hurt probably rendered her too scared to love him again.

The horrible words screamed through her mind again and again like a mental flogging as Mandy drove home.

"I hate you, Nolan."

Where had they come from? How could she have said such a vile, ugly thing? Then he, in the face of her loose-cannon rage, merely cast a tender expression and the excruciatingly tranquil words:

"See, that's the difference between you and me, Mandy. You did stop loving me. You just said so yourself." He'd risen and turned toward the counseling center as if seeking refuge, pausing at the door to face her once more:

"I never stopped loving you, Mandy. Never."

She'd stared at his back as he slipped into his temporary office at the counseling center, allowing her a glimpse of a vulnerability she had only seen a few times in his life.

Now, his open words echoed in her ears like the soft click of his closed door.

I never stopped loving you.

Did that mean he still loved her to this day? That he'd loved her all this time?

Talk about a bombshell.

Vinyl cushions creaked as the weakening in Mandy's legs dictated she lower herself to the couch or end up a pile of slump on the floor.

He still loved her. And had all these years, yet she never

knew it. For a decade she'd believed a lie and hurt over something that wasn't true. Believing he'd rejected and abandoned her and hadn't really ever loved her. Why? Something wasn't right. Things didn't add up.

What was the missing piece?

And once she found it, what was she going to do about it?

First off, she was going to give Nolan the benefit of the doubt that was ten years past due, and unearth the whole truth.

No matter how bad, it couldn't hurt as much as witnessing agony writhe in Nolan's eyes as he fought to protect her by keeping a decade-old secret hidden.

And the one person who probably possessed the key to the vault was undoubtedly the one person Mandy mistakenly thought she could trust more than anyone.

Mandy yanked her phone from her purse and scrolled to her mother's number. When Marva picked up, a cough preceded her hello.

"Mom, I am going to ask you a question. And I need you to tell me the truth. Please."

"Mandy?"

Her mom sounded groggy. She never napped. Which meant she was getting worse. Still, Mandy couldn't let it deter her.

"Mom, please. Just listen. Did Nolan ever, ever call or write to me when he left ten years ago?"

Another cough and a wheeze that caused alarm.

"Mom, are you all right?"

"Oh, Mandy…" A resolute sigh. Then a moist sniff. "First, let me answer your initial question."

"Briggs, someone's here to see you." Aaron Petrowski swept up the parachute harness clip mechanism Nolan was demonstrating to a tandem jumper. "I got this."

Nolan wiped his hands off and entered the DZ lobby to find the shock of his life.

Mandy's mother stood behind the counter. "Nolan."

"Marva." Fighting anger, he approached cautiously. "What brings you to Refuge again?"

She motioned toward a booth near a wall of floor-to-ceiling windows, similar to an airport's, where parachutists could be seen practicing body posture formations on the ground that would be used in the air.

"The biggest mistake of my life brought me. I'm here to make amends." She sat.

Bewilderment toiling with him, Nolan propped his hip against the table. "Mandy know you're here?"

"Not yet." Her hands wrung in her lap.

Anger pressed his hands into the table until his fingers blanched. "She know about the way you—"

"Yes. In fact, she called very angry."

He jerked up. "You told her?"

"No. She figured it out on her own that the pastor and I went behind her back and threatened to end her college funding if you stayed and pursued a relationship with her."

His fist hit the table. It rattled. Marva jerked and he instantly felt bad. Nolan bent his head to try and temper his reaction.

When he rose, tears streaked down Marva's cheeks. Her very sunken cheeks.

"That's not the only reason you're here." A sense of dread climbed all over him.

"No." Her face paled and for the first time since her arrival, Nolan noticed gaunt circles beneath her eyes and how baggy her clothes were since she was here last. She didn't look like she weighed over a hundred pounds. Her skin had a yellowish cast to it.

Concern and awareness filtered through him. "You're worse."

A humility he'd never seen in her before cloaked her eyes about the time her face turned a blustery red and her composure shattered. "Yes. Very much."

Like Mandy, he'd never seen Marva cry.

He sat, breath billowing out. "I'm listening."

"I'm here to ask your forgiveness, and Mandy's. When she called, she told me you'd given your life to God. It brought front and center the mistakes I made ten years ago when I beat the Bible over your head."

Much as he didn't want to, he laughed. "Not literally."

Relief trickled over her face. "Well, at times I wanted to. We attended a legalistic church, Nolan. As new Christians ourselves, we made the mistake of trying to force our faith down your throat. I realize now it probably hindered you more than helped." Her voice broke. She tugged a tissue from her wallet. "I'm humbly sorry. We should have tried to love you to the Lord instead of lead you by angry iron fists."

"You're forgiven. And, for what it's worth, I always knew it was because you loved her and wanted what was best and right and good for her."

"But the way the pastor who provided her scholarship and I went about things was far from good and right and best. And now Mandy knows the hideous things I've done, and I'm not sure she will ever forgive me."

"You intercepted all my letters, didn't you?"

Her head bowed and she ripped tiny particles off the tissue until she'd obliterated it. "Yes. And I changed our phone number and had it unlisted to keep you from contacting her."

"Why?"

"I saw how strong your love was."

The thought to lean across the table and choke her crossed his mind. Guilt over her illness quelled the urge. He leaned back and sighed. "Does she know?"

"Not about the letters."

He stood. "Then we have to go talk to her. Right now."

She grasped his hand. "Nolan, wait. That's not all. I—I don't have much time."

"When do you fly out?"

She looked momentarily startled. Then her expression cleared. "I meant I don't have much time…to live."

Shocked, he slid back down, slowly. "Are you sure?"

"Yes." Hurt lashed like it pained her to say it.

"What—?"

"The cancer metastasized everywhere. Including my liver." She plucked her yellowish-orange skin. "Obviously."

A raw place in his throat made swallowing difficult. "How long?"

"A year. Maybe two."

Nolan dropped his face into his hands, surprised to find tears covering his palms. As much as they'd battled during his adolescence, Marva was still Mandy's mom. And, by some miracle, still someone he cared about.

"Mandy know?"

"She does about the cancer. Just not that it's all over the place now. Nor the grave prognosis."

He raised his head. "We need to tell her." He took her hand.

"I—I'd rather wait. I'm tired. I need to rest and take my medicine. The flight and this meeting with you drained me. Couldn't we wait until tom—"

"No. You need to reconcile." He grabbed her carry-on. "Right now." She and Mandy needed to make the most of every moment they had left together. "Come on, Marva."

"Briggs, where you headed?" Joel intercepted them at the door.

"With Marva to talk to Mandy."

Joel frowned. "It's Monday, bud. Did you forget about the—?"

Nolan's eyes jerked to his watch. "Man! I forgot about the benefit planning meeting today." He was subbing for Petrowski.

Wariness marched across his team leader's eyes. He couldn't let Petrowski down. "I'll be there."

Nolan pulled Marva aside. "I'm sorry. I have a meeting I need to leave for in twenty minutes. Can't miss." He felt torn in two. But, after all, she really did look tired. He thought maybe she'd just been trying to put off the inevitable. But her emotional meeting with Nolan undoubtedly took a lot out of her. She could use time to recoup. "What about tomorrow, after you've rested?"

She nodded. "Tomorrow's fine."

"Or you can go it alone."

"I'd like you to go with me."

Something softened in him. "I'd like that, too. For all our sakes." He scribbled the B and B address on a napkin. "Go here. Tell the landlord you need a room. I'll call on the way and tell her to put it on my rent bill."

"Nolan, I can't ask you to—"

"Yes, you can." He grinned. "After all, I want to stay in the good graces of my future mother-in-law."

Her eyes beamed. "Are you?"

"No. Far from it. At the moment, she can't stand me."

"You two always did have your tiffs."

"Well, this one's big enough that only God Himself can referee it and work it out. However, I did, in faith, purchase a custom-made Panda ring."

For the first time that day, color came to her face. She stood on tippy-toes and clapped. "I pray He does work it out. She will cherish that ring. And you. For what it's worth, I'm ten years late saying this, but I know you'll take good care of her."

"Yes, ma'am. I will in God's time. But, right now, I need to take care of my team." Nolan started outside to find someone to give her a ride to the bed-and-breakfast.

"Oh?" concern etched her features as they passed rosebushes.

"Refuge city council is hosting a benefit for victims of the bridge collapse. The first planning meeting is today. They asked for one representative from the Pararescue team, one from

River Guard divers and one from the flight crews and ambulance teams to represent rescuers that were present. All proceeds will benefit the victims of the collapse. Today is the first meeting and Petrowski was chosen as the committee member to represent the PJs. One of his twins is ill. So he asked me to go in his place since I was in charge on the bridge that day."

"I understand. Now, quit yammering and go do your job. When I kick off, I'll donate some life insurance to the cause."

"Don't talk like that. We'd rather have you around than your money." Nolan led her to the side of the building.

"It was a joke. If I can't kid, I might as well die."

"Marva, don't say such things."

"Nolan, I'm trying to make light of things. If I lose my laughter, my soul dies. If I lose my life, my laughter lives on."

He got it.

Her humor was meant for others. To dwell in their hearts through God's gift of memories. Remembrance. Those who would need as many happy memories as possible to cling to once she was gone. He grew sick at the thought of Mandy finding out. Tomorrow morning was Tuesday. He'd take Marva to the coffeehouse where Mandy and Amelia met once a week. He'd call Ben to keep Reece.

Chance stood at the side, refilling hummingbird feeders in the DZ garden area.

"Garrison, can you break free? Give her a ride to the B and B?"

Chance nodded toward him and smiled at Marva.

"Thanks, bud."

"Nolan, there's one more thing," Marva said, walking him out to the parking lot. She retrieved a hat box from her tote. A sense of foreboding hit him as she tugged off the lid and pulled a cloth-wrapped packet out.

Recognition flared and scorn, until he remembered how much he'd been forgiven for, too. "The letters. You still have them?"

She nodded and handed them over. "She should have had these years ago. So, please hand-deliver them this time."

Only borrowed grace could explain why Nolan's anger didn't resurge over Marva's actions. *Thank you.*

Nodding at Chance, Nolan hugged Marva and left to get into his formal uniform before going to the benefit planning meeting at Refuge City Hall.

Thought about swinging by Square Beans for a stiff shot of espresso. But stomach distress over Marva kept him from it. Queasiness over what Mandy may be facing.

Chapter Nineteen

"Unbelievable," Mandy muttered.

Decked out in formal Air Force dress, Nolan strode in, turning the head of every female at the benefit planning committee table. Every one of them would invade their chiropractor's office for whiplash treatment this week.

She quelled the urge to toss her pen across the room. Instead, she glared at Dr. Riviera's oblivious slick black head as if he'd done this on purpose.

Of course Nolan would be here. He'd been everywhere else she had the past three months.

Nolan looked up then. A startled expression crossed his features as he noticed her while seating himself near the door.

Yeah, right.

He'd probably found out she was on the committee and therefore inserted himself somehow, too.

But a sliver of doubt crept in when he eyed her with sick dread and darted his face away, swallowing hard.

He even paled.

What on earth?

Mandy turned her attention to the people in the front of the room setting up slides while others brought in refreshments.

Rustling next to her pulled her attention to her left.

"Excuse me," Nolan said to the Refuge River Guard woman beside Mandy. "May I trouble you to switch seats with me?"

"Sure, no problem." She rose and claimed his seat.

After slipping to the refreshment table he came back. Slowly. As if a planet sat on his shoulders. Palming two cups, Nolan sat. A strange tension replaced the easy smile usually present in his eyes. His normally agile motions seemed fidgety as he set one of the beverages in front of her. And yes, it was what she would have chosen for herself.

Angling away, Mandy glued malevolent eyes to the aging mayor who approached the podium. "We'll get started in about ten minutes, ladies and gentlemen. Thank you for coming. Feel free to help yourself to refreshments while we wait for others to arrive."

She sipped her coffee until she tasted that he'd made it just like she liked it.

She pushed the cup away.

His breath smelled of peppermint as Nolan leaned over. "Hey. I didn't know you were gonna be here. I'm standing in for Petrowski. He's tied up with his little ones." His apologetic expression convinced her he was sincere.

Guilt waggled a finger at her for thinking earlier that he'd planned this. "You and I keep running into each other."

"Yeah, I noticed that, too." He sent her a wry smile. "So maybe Someone's trying to tell us something."

She stiffened. "Wouldn't know. I don't talk to Him much anymore, either."

He looked no less stricken than if a whip had lashed from her lips. "What's happened to your faith, Mandy?"

"Since when do you care about faith, Nolan?"

"Since I gave my heart to God. Prayers you prayed and all those seeds you planted finally came to fruition."

"Hmmm." But she felt a twinge of something deep. A

gaping hole that couldn't be filled unless she made her way back to God. "How ironic. Just about the time you walk toward God, I run away."

"Why, Mandy? What happened?" he asked softly, a pained expression taking over his face. She was glad he'd whispered because she didn't want strangers into her business. Still, her heart squeezed with her own hostile words.

"Why?" He repeated the question, needing the answer like a heart needed blood pressure.

In boot camp, he'd missed her so much he'd turned to God to fill the void. And learned from many of the enlisted Christians that one didn't need to be at a crux or crisis to turn to God. But for Nolan it was the inciting incident that pushed him into God's arms. He might not be as vocal about this faith as the other guys, but he knew God. Since the team, he'd recovered his faith. And she'd lost hers. It broke his heart above comprehension.

He felt responsible.

"Where did your strong faith go, Mandy?" Nolan whispered, studying her face. Probed deep in her eyes, looking for any microscopic cell of the love he remembered her living and breathing so completely and passionately.

For God. For him.

Nothing. All he could find was a deep hollow. A dark void in her cold eyes.

And it was his fault.

"I lost it the day you left." Her words said "left" but her eyes spoke "abandoned." He'd seen it in her eyes the day his bus had rumbled away from the curb, leaving her looking utterly alone.

If he'd had any idea how it would have wounded her, he wouldn't have enlisted. Would have stayed liked she begged. Or taken her with him. Tried to work things out. But in the end they'd loved each other enough to want what was best for the other more than for themselves. There'd been no other way. Neither one of their families had money to send them to college with and Nolan hadn't applied himself in school to earn scholarships.

None of that mattered now. This was worse than breaking her heart. He'd devastated her faith. Not at all the outcome that he or anyone around them would have expected.

He determined to step up his efforts to help her get back on track with her faith. A tricky thing considering he still needed to give 110 percent to his team. Somehow, he'd conjoin the two missions. Somehow God would make it work.

Help me, help her.

A vague notion formed from oblique edges of his mind and grew sharper.

Thank you.

"Come to church with me, Mandy."

"Not on your life."

"Come to church and I'll donate my savings to the children's free health screening you want to start."

"You'd do that anyway, Nolan. You've always been generous. Undoubtedly more so, now that you know God."

"You're probably right." A sinking feeling hit him that this rescue of her faith was going to be much more difficult than he ever dreamed. This had moved from rescue to recovery.

Mandy's faith was dead in the murky water. Not just dead. Decayed a decade until it had petrified to stone.

As the meeting called to order and droned on, Nolan battled between listening to the presenters and fretting about Marva's terminal cancer and telling Mandy.

He hurt in his gut to sit here beside her knowing tomorrow would forever change and turbine her life into another tailspin.

The revelation he feared would spiral her down further into trauma's undertow, or worse, obliterate her faith again.

And his leaving had been the reason for her fall. Sure, she

had the choice to let adversity push her toward God or pull her away. She had a choice but he still felt responsible.

Another wave of nausea accosted him over the knowledge he possessed and she didn't about her mother.

Would her fragile faith shatter once she knew?

Nolan clenched his fist around the cup and mentally prepared to go to war for the woman he loved.

He might not be able to recover the lost years. But he would do everything he could to rescue her downed faith.

Refuge lived up to its name. Like his team, the Christians in his life knew what it meant to battle. In prayer. He'd enlist their help, their prayers.

Bold and brave and unrelenting until the mission was done.

Just as Joel prayed "help us bring them home" before missions for every pilot shot down behind enemy lines, Nolan sent mental pleas skyward.

Help us. Bring her home.

Chapter Twenty

"So the meeting last night went well, I take it?" Amelia swirled her wooden stir stick around her coffee at Square Beans the next day.

Mandy shrugged. "Well as could be expected with Nolan there."

Amelia's face brightened and her torso rose. "He was?"

"You seem entirely too excited."

Rather than comment, Amelia's eyes widened. She sat abruptly and crooked a finger behind Mandy. "Speaking of…"

Mandy turned just as Nolan, tugging sunglasses off and scanning the room, entered the coffeehouse with…*her mother?*

Shock fizzed through her at how emaciated her mom was. And so starkly pale. Mandy stood. "Mom?"

Why was she here with Nolan? Why was she here, period?

It hit her.

Her phone call.

They hadn't gotten off the phone on good terms at all. Now Marva was here.

The look in her mother's and Nolan's eyes as they found her hinted of more. Mandy'd been too upset to ask her mom about the cough. Overdoses of guilt assailed her. Mandy fought hyperventilation. "Something is wrong." Overcome with sudden weakness, Mandy sagged back and reached for the table. Lowered herself down when her mom caught sight of her and managed a feeble smile.

But not Nolan. His eyes held the deepest fissure of compassion she'd ever seen.

"Mind if we sit?" Marva asked once she and Nolan got to the table. "There are things, hard things, I have to say."

Standing, Amelia searched their faces. "Do I need to leave?"

Mandy reached for her hand. "No. Please don't."

Nolan pulled a chair close to Mandy and rested his hand on her forearm. *Oh, God. This isn't gonna be good.*

Mandy sat back, clunky and stoic and not even wanting to nod.

Marva's jaundice and drastic weight loss, and Nolan's wary, empathetic gaze, it not only wasn't going to be good, it was going to be very, very bad.

"Mom, tell me what's going on." Mandy trembled.

They retreated to a quiet and comfortable lounge area. Everyone settled in and Marva took Mandy's hands in hers, careful with the one she'd broken.

"First off, Mandy, I'm sorry for sabotaging your and Nolan's communication ten years ago."

Mandy's lip trembled. "It's okay." But it wasn't.

But she couldn't concern herself with that right now. Something else took precedence. "M-mom. What's happening with your health?"

The doctor in her saw the jaundice and pallor and weight loss and wanted to ask how poor the prognosis was.

But the little girl in Mandy wanted to climb in her mom's lap and cry because she knew it wasn't good.

Looking close to desperate, Marva looked to Nolan. So strange to see her mother interact with Nolan, whom she used to look at with contention. But her expression held a desolate plea.

Nolan drew a breath. "Mandy, she has terminal cancer."

"I knew it." Mandy blinked from one to the other. "Mom, please don't tell me you're dying."

Marva's hand came to her mouth, then to clutch Mandy's hand. "I wish I weren't."

Mandy's stomach dipped then fell into something bottomless. Her mind reeled. Her legs grew shaky and her arms numbed. Her mind spun. "No. You can't."

Marva broke down and Mandy fell into her open arms.

Later, after it settled in, the more they shared about the type and the prognosis, the more Mandy felt like throwing up.

Marva stood. "Nolan, I need a word with you privately."

She all but dragged him to the other side of the shop.

In their absence, Amelia came close. "I won't even ask if you're okay."

"Something in me can't accept this. Much trouble as me and her had getting along sometimes, I don't want to lose her."

"I know." Amelia wrapped an arm around Mandy's shoulder.

A latte later, her mom and Nolan returned. His face gave nothing of the hidden conversation away. But Marva looked more relieved.

"There are experimental treatments," Mandy said to her.

"Do I look like a science experiment, Mandy?"

"Not yet. But you will if you sign that donate-your-body-to-science paper. Which you are not going to do by the way because we are getting a second opinion."

"Mandy, I've gotten a second and a third and a fourth opinion. They're all the same."

Shoulders heaving and face in her hands, Mandy broke down. "You've given up."

Nolan sustained her with his arms as best he could. She trembled all over.

More courageous than he'd seen her a minute ago, Marva lifted Mandy's face. "I have not."

Good. Marva was trying to be strong for Mandy. She did love her daughter.

Marva gave a grand sweep of her arms. "In fact, I'm taking up skydiving next Thursday. A week from today. Nolan's taking me."

"You're not serious?" Mandy's neck craned.

"I certainly am. And I'm not strapping myself to anyone either. I'm jumping out of that plane all by myself."

Mandy stood. "You can't!"

Marva straightened and it was like looking at a mirror of two identically charged women stuck in separate generations. "Just why not?"

"You've never done it."

"So?"

"Well, you'll kill yourself!" Mandy clamped a hand over her mouth.

Amelia gave a choking sound.

Nolan dipped his head.

Marva rolled her head back. And laughed. Then again, so hard her mouth was open but no sound except rhythmic hissing from her throat came out.

Arms wrapped around her stomach, a fit of giggles hit Mandy.

Slowly, it trickled around the circle until it had embraced each of them.

Mandy wiped her eyes. "I can't believe we're laughing at a time like this. Mom, when did you get such a sense of humor?"

"Since the day I found out I was dying. So I laugh about everything I can because I want to live as long as I have left."

"Mom, don't—"

"Mandy, listen. Some way, somehow, somewhere in the world tomorrow someone's mom will die. And the day after that. And so on into next week and beyond."

Mandy looked stricken. Nolan squeezed her shoulder.

"Granted, likely not me if your boyfriend and his adrenaline-addicted friends actually know what they're doing."

Mandy's cheeks tinged. "He's not my—" But she stopped, giving him hope.

"Mothers will die tomorrow, Mandy. In a car crash. In the blink of an eye. Or with family surrounded, giving her soul permission to go because she's suffered so hard and so long and it's her God-appointed time and they know it."

"No, Mom!" Mandy sobbed. "Stop."

"Mandy, wait. You need to hear this. They'll hold her hand and say goodbye and she'll slowly slip away. A different mother will succumb to death by heart disease or diabetes."

Mandy shook her head. But listened.

"Another mother will die in a natural disaster or in some kind of accident." She laughed feebly. "And that could be me. At the Drop Zone, or in a car on the way there. I almost lost you in a bridge collapse, Mandy. That day was the worst day of my life. I put my house up for sale and I'm moving to Refuge to be near you."

Mandy's face lifted. A mercy-laced smile sprang forth.

Marva drew close. "At least we know to use the time we have left, be it two years or forty. Let's redeem the time and recover the ground we lost." She hugged Mandy and released.

Mandy stood. "Fine. If you're going skydiving next Thursday, then so am I."

Marva blushed. "Then I suppose I should mention that I was embellishing about the going by myself part. I planned to tandem with Nolan. Unless you'd rather ride with him?"

"No way. I want to be strapped to the video guy so I can see you scream your guts out."

Nolan settled on the armrest next to Mandy. "I hate to break the news, but no one can be strapped to the videographer during a dive."

Marva checked her watch and stood. "Then she can ride with you from the plane to the earth and from earth through this life until Heaven, Nolan. I will never break the two of you up again."

Thankful relief shuttled over Nolan because Mandy was forgiving Marva, and Marva had been able to admit how wrong she'd been.

He'd invited her to tomorrow night's barbecue and hoped she'd come. The more time she and Mandy spent together, the better.

Marva strode out looking stronger than when she came. Amelia followed, leaving Nolan and Mandy alone.

Mandy's jaw hung open. Nolan pressed her chin so it closed. "Okay?"

"I have never seen her like this." She searched his face. "I—I've missed you."

He grinned.

"And, I found your note."

His grin faded. He drew a deep breath. "And?"

"You've got a point. But before I make it, I have a question."

His brows rose and he almost laughed.

"What was the number 157 all about?"

He swallowed. "That was before…before you knew about the interceptions."

Understanding dawned. "That's how many notes you'd written."

"Yes. I sent you a letter every week for three solid years. Then I stopped. Figured it was no use. I hadn't received a reply for 156 weeks. Didn't figure I ever would." *I lost hope.*

"But you figured wrong."

He nodded. "Your mom kept all the notes. She gave them to me yesterday. I read them last night."

A breath shuddered out of her. "C-can I read them, too?"

"Of course. They were meant for you."

She nodded.

"Keep in mind I meant everything I said. And more." He brushed the back of his hand along her cheek. "Especially the last one. About God."

Something glittered in her eyes. Not tears this time. Resolve. "I know. I also know you're exactly right."

"So, you'll go with me on real dates then?"

She smiled. "Be delighted and honored to accompany such a hunk."

"You're bringing Mooch then, I take it?"

She smiled demurely. "I'm talking about you."

"I know." He bumped her shoulder in an intimate gesture. "But I just wanted to hear you say it. By the way, I invited Marva to the Friday night barbecues but she said she needs to go home for a few weeks. Know what she said to me over there?"

"What did she say?"

"I'll tell you after you tell me what she said to you when the two of you visited the restroom."

"She said, 'I want you to promise me you will try to work things out with him. Even if I don't live to see your wedding day.'"

He paused, hand on her forearm.

Mandy laughed. "I couldn't focus really on the part about you because I was too busy throwing myself in her arms and crawling in her lap and begging her not to die. I'm a real dish, huh?"

"Yeah." The one he wanted served for life. "And by the way, no matter how old we are, we're never ready to let them go."

"I'm sorry you lost your mom so young, Nolan."

"Me, too." Something twinkled beneath her shirt collar. He leaned in. The panda necklace. "You put it back on?"

She nodded and a smile twitched about her mouth. "Things never felt right without it. I'll never take it off again."

He scratched his temple. "Uh, that's great. But can I borrow it for a few days?"

A perplexed look came over her but she shrugged and removed it, handing it to him. It felt cool in his hand. Now he could take it to the jeweler making Mandy's surprise engagement ring, so the two jewel-embedded pandas could be more closely matched.

He smiled inside, knowing he'd propose Thursday as soon as their feet hit solid earth. Or, better yet, he'd have the team write a message on the Drop Zone floor. Nah. That wouldn't work because rain was in the forecast. He'd think of a way before Thursday that she could read from air or ground.

An idea struck.

He grinned. The message he'd waited ten years to ask her. *Manda Panda, Marry Me?*

Nolan was silly with anticipation as he pulled up in his truck to pick up Mandy for Refuge's Bridge Benefit. This was an official date between them and he looked forward to being alone with her.

Before he could get out of the car, Ivy Manor's door opened. Mandy and Miss Ivy walked the path toward the car. Momentary disappointment groaned inside Nolan when he realized Mandy, in her soft-heartedness, had probably offered a ride to Miss Ivy. His own compassion trumped over his want to have Mandy to himself. He got out and opened the door. "Evening, ladies."

Miss Ivy peered up as he lent a hand to help her step up onto the running board of his truck. "Nolan, I hope I'm not intruding."

Of course you are. "No, Ma'am. We're glad to give you a ride." Truthfully, as good as Mandy looked tonight, it was probably best they weren't all that alone.

What was it about her that looked more appealing than usual?

She wore more makeup and sparkly panda earrings. Shorts that showcased long, lean legs. Or maybe it was the Air Force blue top that brought out her eyes and curves he probably shouldn't notice so intently. Or maybe it was just because he knew without a doubt she was becoming his.

But, wow, those high-wedge sandals and the way they made her legs look really did him in. He cleared his suddenly dry throat and tore his unruly eyes away.

Chattering to Miss Ivy and oblivious to his approving assessment, Mandy climbed in the truck next. He held her hand long enough for her words to stutter as she searched his gaze. He grinned and helped her the rest of the way in. "Hi, beautiful."

Now her cheeks matched ruby lips and eyes normally lined with intelligence turned endearingly shy. "Hi."

Miss Ivy kept the communication ball in the air all the way to the town square, where the benefit was to be held. Good thing, too, because Nolan sensed Mandy was as aware of him as he was of her. Thank God He'd sent a chaperone.

Miss Ivy exited, then waved. "Toodles, you two. I've got to go man the knitting booth. Have fun!" And she was off.

When Mandy climbed out, a childlike anticipation entered her eyes. "Wow. Look at this."

Nolan eyed their surroundings. Sounds of small town carnival rides filled the air. Food and goodie vendors' trucks and booths lined both sides of the main street in Refuge for blocks. "The town is transformed."

Mandy took Nolan's hand as they walked toward a lemon and orange shake-up booth. "Thank you for all your hard work, Nolan. This benefit will be a healing thing for the victims' families and the town."

He nodded. "You put a lot of hours in, too. And I'm glad to share the results of our labor with you." He squeezed her hand before tugging out his wallet. "Lemon or orange?"

"What do you think?" She winked.

He placed bills on the counter. "She'll have orange and I'll have lemon."

Next they moved to the cotton candy and taffy booth. They sat across from one another. Mandy started to pluck downy pink fuzz from the cardboard cone when Nolan slipped it from her hand. He finger fed her bites until she held her hand out, waving.

He turned. Then stood to meet their friends. "Hey Ben, Amelia." He rustled Hutton's and Reece's heads, then tickled Bearby, Reece's stuffed animal, on its lopsided, threadbare body.

"You guys wanna do rides?" Ben pulled out bracelets he must have purchased for the occasion.

"I haven't ridden carnival rides since I was a kid," Mandy said.

Nolan tugged her toward the amusement park section. "Then it's about time you did."

Of course she knew he'd head straight for the Ferris wheel as soon as darkness hinted. The twinkle in his eye told her he remembered very well they used to steal kisses on the top of it during their high school summers when they were sure her mom wasn't looking.

Speaking of, Mandy suddenly missed her. Nolan must have seen the change in her face. "You okay?"

"Yeah. Just miss Mom is all. I can't get over feeling like there's more they can do for her."

"She promised to inquire about experimental treatment."

"I know. But that she hasn't called makes me concerned."

"When did you speak with her last?" Nolan directed her to the back of the Ferris wheel line.

Mandy waved at Amelia, Ben, Hutton and Reece who were halfway up the line. "Yesterday. But she didn't sound herself. Sounded really out of it. Fatigued to the point she was almost incoherent. She's going downhill fast."

"If we don't hear from her in the next couple of days, we'll drive there to see her. Okay?"

"Thank you, Nolan."

"It's got to be frustrating to be a healer yet feel like your hands are tied when it comes to family."

Mandy nodded.

"I'll go with you to see your Mom whenever you want."

She shifted and looked away. "Okay."

He clasped her hand and moved into her line of vision. "But?"

"But what?"

"Something's wrong. In you, I mean. You sorta shut down on me there for a second."

She brushed hair over her shoulder. "Yeah. I guess I kinda feel like we're slipping back into old patterns."

"What do you mean?"

"I mean you always felt the need to rescue me."

"You had a lot of anxiety as a teen. And rightfully so with your father abandoning you and your mother, then her sort of taking it out on you. It put you nearly alone."

She shrugged. "You still see me as weak?"

He shook his head. "No. That's absolutely not true. Your PTSD as an adult was partly triggered by that trauma in your teens. You were a child then. Your parents' choices are not your fault, Mandy, nor the fallout from them. Do you understand what I'm telling you?" The ride line moved up. They kept in step.

She licked her lips. "I'm not sure."

"Then let me spell it out." He bent to kiss her in front of God and everyone. Made her feel as if her world was a planet-sized Ferris wheel and she was right on top. He put his hands on her shoulders and looked deep into her eyes.

"Mandy, you are a strong woman who happens to have PTSD."

"It felt like you were trying to take over my life. Because you feel sorry for me."

He laughed. "I feel sorry only that you feel that way. I feel far from sorry for you, Manda Panda. You are a strong, capable woman and an outstanding doctor. You can take care of yourself and you *will* get better."

She had to know. "Are you hanging around just to be sure of that? You've always been a rescuer, Nolan."

He bent in. "I really want to kiss you again, but little children are watching."

Her face heated.

He lowered his eyelids and his face to whisper. "The reason I'm hanging around is because I love spending time with you. Laughing. Talking. Interacting." His gaze dropped to her mouth.

Kissing. "I love being with you. I want to be with you. I don't like the thought of being without you."

"Me, too."

But there was something deeper happening here than a much-needed, long-longed-for profession of their love. The knowledge that God's heart was coming through Nolan expanded hope inside.

But would their careers once again be the catalyst that careened them in opposite directions?

"I can't ask her," Nolan said the next day seated in front of Joel at the DZ. "Not when that could mean we have to choose each other over our careers and vice versa."

Joel's deep chuckle brought warmth. "Nolan, I've not been praying my heart out for you and Mandy for months only to have you pull something as stupid as waiting when the time is right now. Plus she'll want her mom to witness the wedding. Trust God to work out the details."

"I will." Nolan eyed Vince, who for once didn't flinch at the mention of God.

In fact, he was first to step forward. "Congrats, man. Happy for ya." The normally dark, brooding Vince clapped a hand on Nolan's shoulder, then stepped back with a wide grin that said he was as happy about this as Nolan.

Then his entire team followed suit with congratulatory words and gestures.

Nolan stood and shook each of their hands. "Thanks. I just needed to hear you guys say it."

Aaron Petrowski pressed Nolan's back. "I've good news to add. Superiors okayed our proposal to expand the local PJ programs, Nolan. Which means the superiors are likely to keep you stationed here in Refuge."

Thankfulness consumed Nolan. Though he'd serve his country any way necessary, he sure was glad to serve with this group of honorable men—his closest friends. "Thanks, Chief. I appreciate you pulling for me to stay with the team."

Petrowski shook his hand. "Now, go get the girl. We'll see you at the barbecue."

"Yo, dude. When you gonna ask her?" Vince fiddled with his motorcycle helmet.

"Thought about asking her when we take her and Marva skydiving Thursday. If you guys could help me rig up a banner big enough for her to read from ground or the air."

"You got a ring?" Vince asked.

"Yeah. A sterling silver one shaped like a panda."

"How many diamonds?"

"Eight. One for the body. One for the head. Two for the ears. And four for the arms and legs. And two black onyx stones for the eyes."

"Dude, she'll set airport security off with that thing. How many carats?"

"Enough that I gotta jump every day this year in order to pay it off." Nolan laughed even though he was serious. "But hey, what a way to win her heart." He wiggled his fingers sideways in a cool trick Manny's teen son taught him. "See you birds at the barbecue."

"Yo, Briggs!" Vince followed him out. "Mandy be there?"

"Always."

Vince hopped on his Harley and displayed a rakish grin. "Can I ask her to dance when Ben plays his guitar?"

"Never."

Vince laughed and fired up his custom-built bike.

A thought struck Nolan. "Hey!"

Vince kicked out the stand. "Yeah?"

"Make you a deal. You stay for Ben's singing, and I'll let you have the first dance at the wedding."

His face lit up. "With your sweetheart?"

"No. With me." Nolan smirked. "Of course with Mandy. Only she'll be my wife then."

"Sounds like coercion to me. But I'll think about it."

Nolan stood staring after Vince for ten solid minutes after the gravel dust from his bike dissipated.

Manny came out to get in his truck. "Dude, you still here?"

"Yeah. Vince is thinking about not cutting out early."

Manny's dark eyes bugged. "He staying for the worship part?"

"I think so." Though he didn't want to get his hopes up too much.

Looking dazed, Manny shook his head. "There is a God."

"As if you ever doubted."

Manny grew serious. "Actually, I did. Remember where I was a few years ago, Briggs. And look where I am now. And know there's hope for Brock and Chance and Vince." Manny stepped up into his truck but leaned his torso out. "And Mandy."

Nolan stepped closer. "Appreciate you and Joel and Ben and your families praying for her."

"Unceasing." Manny draped his dark arm across the top of the door. "Takes time, bud. Worst thing you can do is run in front of God and rush 'em."

And no one knew that better than Nolan.

Chapter Twenty-One

"Mandy's responding surprisingly well," Dr. Riviera said to Nolan at the Friday barbecue the following evening. "She'll be released back to duty soon."

And hopefully, into his arms, too. He hadn't gotten to spend as much time with her today but he'd stayed busy with his team while Mandy and her mother pursued every medical avenue to treat Marva's cancer.

"I hope Marva responds well, too."

"I'm glad Joel and Amber referred her to you. You being Bradley's cancer doctor and such."

Mandy, in a huddle of children, dogs and a crazy cat, ran across the yard in some kind of bouncy ball relay. Children shrieked with laughter and the dogs barked their ecstasy at all the attention.

Riviera chuckled as Mandy tackled teen Enrique, Celia's son Javier's best friend. "She seems to be coping with her mother's news okay."

Nolan nodded. "Seems to."

Joel stood and whistled. "Hey guys, listen up. Ben's getting ready to play."

Nolan cast a sideways glance at Vince who smirked and lifted his beer in a long-distance toast.

"I think he's actually gonna stay," Nolan said about Vince when Joel joined him on the banister near where Ben tuned his acoustic.

Just then, Mandy sidled up next to him. "Hey, handsome." Her perfume caught him off guard and so did her smile.

He almost slipped off the thin board railing. "Hey, gorgeous. You look great."

"Thanks." She started to use her arms to lift herself up beside him.

He jumped down. "Wait." Hands to her waist, he lifted her, then took his place beside her. "Didn't want you to reinjure your hand."

"I know. I keep forgetting about my precautions because it feels so much better. I forget most of the time that I broke it."

"Your mom looks at peace."

She squeezed his arm and a smile lit her face. "I noticed that, too."

He wrapped his arm around her as Ben began to play. Eyes closed, Nolan tuned his mind to God for worship, and prayed God would use Ben's song to reach the ones who didn't yet understand what true worship was all about.

I don't want them to miss out. Nor do I want You to miss out on what You're worthy of. Use Ben's gift as it pleases You. Show them You love them any way You want. Inhabit Your praises. Amen.

Something stirred inside Mandy's heart the moment the music started. It awed her that Ben made up all his own songs. Words drifted forward, and the music made her sway without thinking. She closed her eyes and let the words take hold of her. As strong as Nolan's embrace yet as gentle as a breeze, they wrapped themselves around her.

Something about God singing over them.

"There's nothing about You that we can't love. God above. Dancing Lord, do You really spin on Heaven's floor? Cause You think we're worth dancing for? You sing over us, over us with glee and quiet us with peace. Until we know, You're worth singing for. No words do You justice Lord, but see inside our hearts, they know You're worth so much more, One adored, may we have this dance forever, forever more?"

By the time Ben started the next song Mandy remembered where she'd heard the words. Zephaniah 3:17. Ben was singing scripture songs.

When was the last time her mind recalled obscure Bible verses? Ones she hadn't read in years? During Ben's second song, it all came flooding back. Aspects of her faith that she'd thought long dead.

By the third song, Mandy started dialoguing to Him in her head. Something about Ben's authentic worship called to deep places in her. Sparked memories of times alone in her room at night, playing a worship CD and praying for people.

Even Nolan, whom she sensed beside her even now, lifting his hands up to God. Strange to hear him worship when that's all she'd ever wanted. Something she'd prayed for so long. She had to look. Had to.

She opened her eyes. To see Nolan and his friends was a sight to behold. Even the ones who weren't actively engaged in worship were swaying or gently rocking to the music. Even Vince, beer in one hand, Mooch's leash in the other.

Knowing worship was meant to be about God and not everyone around her, she closed her eyes.

And prayed.

How I've missed You. Missed this. Being with You. Pouring my heart out in honesty.

And she knew He heard. Nowhere in His presence did she feel anything other than kindness, grace and His joyous pleasure over her return.

But remorse for the lost years threatened to push heaving sobs from her gut. She didn't want to cry in front of everyone. Not that they'd care but her pride would. Well, so what, that was about the best thing she could lose right now.

Nonetheless, Mandy felt drawn to be alone with God. That overpowering urge and a rush of all kinds of emotion empowered her. Time to do a complete 180 and make things right. One step away and the first words to Ben's next song became her undoing. The deep sorrow and need that she'd stuffed for so long threatened to gush. Mandy slipped from the rail beside Nolan and stumbled as discreetly as possible toward the edge of the woods.

With every step, sorrow fled and joy took its place. Pulling in the most fulfilling drink of air, she put her hand up against a tree. And smiled. An inner exhilaration that she hadn't experienced in years began to bubble as Ben's new song wafted across the yard. Since she didn't know the words, by heart, Mandy mouthed along.

"It's all coming back. Just like that. One step and You come running, running to rescue me. I'd rather be caught by You than to be set free. To my own way. I'd rather stay. Chained to You than lose everything I know of You. Your presence. Unconditional acceptance. Picking up right where we left off. God of grace. I tried to run. Hide my face. My sin. Nearly did me in. But You didn't walk away. You ran, You wooed, You chased, pursued, stubborn Lord of rescue, You loved until you won. I can come like the chasm never happened. Inside

Your love, knowing it. I am undone. Because of Your Son, I can come. Home again. My soul, my heart, my love, my Lord—You won. So now I run, run and rest myself inside of You, mercy, my haven—Your rescue."

With the last strum, silence filled the yard but praise and adoration rose from Mandy's heart. She knelt to the grass and lifted her face to the sky.

"God, I'm here. Because of Your Son, it can be just like the chasm never happened."

Feeling giggles erupt that she could no longer contain, she stepped deeper into the stand of trees. Wished she had a flashlight. Rapid foot-crunches trailed her. Then a hand on her shoulder. Didn't look to see who. Probably Nolan. Of course Nolan. Torrential tears of joy and wonder and darkness over the yard wouldn't let her see.

Yet things were clearer than they'd been in years.

Nolan had felt Mandy break as soon as Ben started singing that last song. By the end of the first stanza, she'd slipped away and bolted for the trees.

He followed because he didn't want her to get lost in the woods or be embarrassed about crying and miss the rest of worship. He'd caught up to her near the edge of Joel's property.

Reached for her arm. "Mandy. You can come back."

She turned, smile radiant. "I am."

"You are?" It dawned on him what she meant and the greatest rush of relief washed over him. It also dawned on him that she wasn't crying but laughing.

"But I have to do this one alone, Nolan. Just me and Him."

Still stunned, Nolan's feet glued to the earth. "Oh, wow. Okay. Yeah. Of course." He stepped back while that registered and ran into something solid.

Vince.

Nolan faced him but angled so he could still keep an eye on Mandy where she knelt beside a tree to the side of Joel's house. "Hey, Vince."

"Dude, she all right?" Looking uncomfortable, Vince yanked a thumb at Mandy, uncustomary concern evident in his eyes.

For the first time, Nolan noticed he'd hardly touched his beer and his breath didn't hint of ninety-proof anything.

"Yeah, she's gonna be fine." *And so are you if God keeps this up.*

Nolan watched Mandy rise and turn to walk back. Her face held a radiance he hadn't seen since she was younger.

She's back!

Thankful emotion burned Nolan's throat and eyes.

She tucked her arm in his and led him with a new lightness to her steps.

Steps leading her home.

Chapter Twenty-Two

"The first step's a doozey," Nolan said to Mandy as she stared at the way, way, way-down-there ground the next Thursday.

Her mother, tandem clipped to Aaron Petrowski, had already launched from the twin prop plane.

Mandy gasped and clapped as their bright parachute deployed below.

Nolan leaned close. "Our turn."

Mandy braced her hands at the opening. Despite her goggles, the wind howling by made her eyes water and her ears ring.

She refused to be scared though. Today was a new day. And she'd face her future with gladness.

Nolan looked at the gauge on his arm. "Ready?"

"Yes!" Not that he could hear her above the wind and the small plane that looked one step above a crop duster. Mandy nodded and stuck her thumb up.

Nolan pressed her forward and together they fell into a blast of cold, deafening wind. Wind that felt like a wall. Took her breath. Freezing! Nolan motioned above her. Signal. Oh, right.

She positioned her legs correctly and moved her arms out as they'd shown her in the pre-skydiving class. Harder up here than it had been on the ground. But she managed.

How had Joel heard Amber screaming up here? All Mandy could hear was the deafening air and her heart pounding.

Whoosh!

Suddenly, they were floating instead of free-falling. And she could hear again.

She began to giggle. "I always thought you'd have the scary sensation of bottomless falling. But it felt like we were flying on a magic carpet of wind!"

No wonder people get addicted to this! No wonder these adrenaline junkies lived in the clouds! No wonder they did this for a living.

"I love this!"

"And I love you," Nolan said, steering them to the Drop Zone floor. The ground rose to meet them in a gentle glide. Nolan steered the chute like a graceful dancing partner. Their feet touched simultaneously.

People cheered when they finally came to a stop.

Nolan clicked off their tandem parachute.

Vince walked up to her, and laid a white rose, with a black and silver bow at the top of the stem, at her feet.

"What's this?" She picked it up. Then, another one, identical, appeared by her sneakers. She looked up. Brock had a wide grin. Then Chance walked up next and laid a rose at her feet. Then Joel.

"What on earth?" She picked up each rose.

Nolan's entire team lined up and proceeded to give her roses. Where was Nolan? Mandy looked around but couldn't find him.

Another rose was laid at her feet. This time by Ben. Then Aaron. Chance. Manny. Then they all stood back in a military line, grinning, to watch her.

Amelia moved forward. "Look up, Manda-Panda."

She lifted her face. The twin prop engine was back in the air, buzzing along. A sign trailed it. She squinted and read the four words aloud.

"Marry Me, Manda Panda?"

Heart pounding, breath coming up short, her eyes searched around. "Where's Nolan?"

"Right behind you."

She whirled. He stepped through the crowd with the rest of the white bouquet in his arms. Coming inches close, he rested the remaining roses in her arms. Then dropped to one knee. Cameras flashed around her.

"Oh!" Her hand went to her mouth. Happy tears flooded her eyes. Had that proposal message been trailing the plane she jumped from the entire time she was in it?

The thought caused her to laugh.

He swallowed. And she knew without a doubt he was proposing. His face had never looked more vulnerable, or tender.

Or more handsome.

"Mandy." He stayed kneeling and took her hand. He placed the most oddly shaped ring on her finger.

Adjusting her roses to her inner elbow, she lifted it.

"A panda ring!"

He took her hand again and stood, eye to eye. "I promise you that if you'll be my wife, I'll find a way to make our marriage work despite our careers."

He could tell the moment shock and doubt waned and understanding dawned. Mandy's shriek drew the attention of the entire DZ crowd.

"Hey, I think that guy's proposing!" someone shouted out. Cheers and clapping erupted and not just from their close friends, who knew ahead of time. A mob of people converged on them.

"Did she say yes?" someone else asked.

Nolan squeezed Mandy's hand. "Did you?"

She looked like she finally caught her breath. Her feet did a series of little deer-like hops and skips. "Yes!" She leapt and body slammed her new fiancé with ten years' worth of it's-about-time vigor.

Someone pounded Nolan on the back. "Yes! She said yes!"

"Mom!" Mandy let go of Nolan and embraced her mother.

"My baby's getting married!" She shot two fists into the air and danced a jig that would tire her out for days.

The crowd of PJs and their families closed in and cheered and whooped and clapped and hugged. Skydiving customers called their congratulations across the DZ grounds.

"You're really gonna marry me?" Nolan asked, hoping he wasn't in some kind of elaborate dream.

Mandy nodded and hugged Nolan again.

"When?" He hoped soon. Next weekend would be good.

Mandy squeezed Nolan's hand. "As soon as possible. This weekend would be good. Sunday."

Nolan coughed out a laugh. "This weekend? As in, three days?"

Mandy grinned like a loon. "Uh-huh. Elope at the DZ after you take me and Mom skydiving again."

His face brightened, hands tightened around hers. "This Sunday? You're sure?"

"Yes! You know I never wanted anything fancy. Remember when you married me in second grade under the slide? I only had a bathroom paper towel for a veil, a soda tab for a ring and borrowed—okay, stolen—flowers for a bouquet. As long as I have you and a new white skydiving outfit to get married in, that's all I need. Is that okay with you?"

"Even better than the date I had planned."

As he moved in for the kill, she put her finger between their lips. "Before we make it official, I have one request."

He grinned against her finger. "Let me kiss you and I'll agree to anything."

"Agree first."

He dipped his head and laughed. "Woman, for a doctor, you're killing me here. All right, spill."

"I get to have a panda-shaped cake to match my panda

ring. I wear white. You wear black. And I get to name our first three children."

Nolan's brow rose. "Anything else?"

"Yes, matter of fact while I'm at it, I'd like to rename our dog, too."

"I'll agree on one condition...I get to buy you a coffee table."

"If you weren't so cute, I think I'd be offended. But fine." She quelled a snicker.

Side by side now, he slung his arm around her shoulder and they walked in step. He inclined his head. "You really wanna rename the dog?"

She grinned. "Smooch."

Pausing, Nolan dipped his head. "If you insist."

She put one finger between their kiss again. "Smooch is his new name."

"Long as I get to do it every time you say it."

"I think I'm getting the better end of that deal."

"Negative. I'm sure I am."

"I hope this is one argument we always have."

She moved her finger and fell into the bliss of Nolan's kiss.

Afterward, they continued their side-by-side stroll across the DZ. "Where are you taking me?" Mandy asked.

He smiled and eyed the horizon. "You'll see."

He stopped at one of the DZ's grassy knolls and turned her shoulders to face the east.

They had an unobstructed view overlooking Reunion Bridge over Refuge River. Her heart squeezed. A couple of tears, then joy. Especially when she noticed the cranes and other signs of reconstruction. Rebuilding. Restoring. Renovating.

Repairing what was broken. Like the chasm never happened.

She gulped emotion down knowing she'd come full circle. She was almost better, like the bridge. Yet not quite. Yet he still loved her for her. Warmth from his embrace spread over her like the sun. As if God knew she'd been on her way back even before she did. Tears tried to come but smiles won when God's peace consumed her. Nolan held her. She rested firmly in His love but determined she would look to God. Always God. And never completely Nolan to meet her needs.

I get it. Finally.

His face glowed with content, his eyes with intent as he dipped his head. Gently dragged his lips across hers in a delectable dance that sealed their love with firm promise: hope for a future that would hold steady and strong.

Just like the new steel support beams and firm concrete foundation and the prayers of Refuge that hugged and held up the being-newly-rebuilt Reunion Bridge.

* * * * *

Dear Reader,

Not until this book was finished did I realize the strong thread running through it of God reuniting the heroine to Himself. I didn't set out to write a prodigal daughter's return story, but somehow that theme prevailed. I pray you are in solid pursuit of The One who chased you first. Of Jesus, who loved you enough to die to ensure you'd be with Him forever. This book is about romance and happily-ever-after. So is the cross. And so is God. He is the only real hero, who will not rest or relent until you are safely His. Run hard after Him.

If you've ever stepped away, know there is forgiveness. Believe me, I've been there. Done that. Ran hard. Came back.

During the writing of this book, singer Steven Curtis Chapman lost his daughter when his eldest son's SUV struck her in the driveway. In an interview, Steven said when his son realized he'd killed his sister, he ran. Grieving over both children, the father got in his car and chased the son. The entire time the son ran, Steven chased. Leaning out the window driving alongside, he yelled over and over, "Will Franklin, your father loves you!"

This story strikes me profoundly as an image of the mercy of our Father in Heaven. How he responds when we mess up.

If you are running, I pray you can hear Him, stubborn and relentless, calling your name and saying, "Your Father loves you."

Then I pray you run the other way, toward Him.

Please keep the Chapman family, and especially Will Franklin, in your prayers.

I love hearing from readers. I invite you to e-mail me at Cheryl@CherylWyatt.com or to write to me at P.O. Box 2955, Carbondale, Illinois 62902-2955.

Cheryl Wyatt

QUESTIONS FOR DISCUSSION

1. Nolan's and Mandy's careers led them in opposite directions after high school. Do you feel Nolan made the right decision in letting Mandy, his high-school sweetheart, pursue her dream, even though it meant losing her? Please discuss.

2. Mandy's strength came out of the collapsed bridge when she discovered a frightened group of schoolchildren. Do you think her medical training helped in that situation? Or do you feel it was more that God gave her what she needed in that moment?

3. Nolan's military training helped him to recognize signs of post-traumatic stress disorder in Mandy after the wreck. Do you think he was right in being so open about his concern? Why or why not?

4. Mandy felt Nolan was trying to reinsert himself back into her life by planting reminders of the time they were together a decade ago. Do you think Nolan was in the wrong here? Or do you agree that he was simply trying to be considerate of her likes and dislikes?

5. Through the bridge collapse, Mandy's prayers were answered in that she met a woman named Amelia who befriended her. Being new in town, Mandy longed for female friendships. How important do you think friendships are for women?

6. The fictional town of Refuge created a benefit for its bridge-collapse victims. In my WINGS OF REFUGE series, Refuge is known as a place that lives up to its name. In what ways did Refuge do that in this story?

7. Nolan got Mandy a dog. Do you think animals can be good therapy for people suffering emotional and physical challenges? Why or why not? Do you think the dog helped Mandy? If so, in what way?

8. What do you think triggered Mandy's turning point as far as her being willing to give her heart back to Nolan? Do you think his kindness had anything to do with her softening?

9. Nolan was determined to restore Mandy's lost faith. He's a rescuer by nature. Do you think this is a reflection of God?

10. Does Mandy, in her faltering faith, remind you of anyone in your life? If so, whom? And what do you think it was that caused them to walk away? As Nolan did, have you determined to pray for that person until they return, no matter how long it takes? Why or why not?

11. Mandy's dream since childhood was to be a doctor. Are you glad she realized her dream? Do you think God gives us the dream first? Or the will to follow it? Which hopes have you realized? And which one are you still waiting for? Did this story encourage you that God is in control? If so, how?

12. The Bible says that deferred hope makes the heart sick. Mandy was devastated when she had to give up Nolan to develop the God-given talent that led to her becoming a

doctor. Yet ten years later, they met again on Reunion Bridge. Do you think that God can really work circumstances out this meticulously? Or do you tend to lean toward thinking things are coincidental?

When a tornado strikes a small Kansas town, Maya Logan
sees a new, tender side of her serious boss. Could a family
man be lurking beneath Greg Garrison's gruff exterior?

Turn the page for a sneak preview of their story in
HEALING THE BOSS'S HEART
by Valerie Hansen,
Book 1 in the new six-book
AFTER THE STORM
miniseries
available beginning July 2009
from Love Inspired®.

Maya Logan had been watching the skies with growing concern and already had her car keys in hand when she jerked open the door to the office to admit her boss. He held a young boy in his arms. "Get inside. Quick!"

Gregory Garrison thrust the squirming child at her. "Here. Take him. I'm going back after his dog. He refused to come in out of the storm without Charlie."

"Don't be ridiculous." She clutched his arm and pointed. "You'll never catch him. Look." Tommy's dog had taken off running the minute the hail had started.

Debris was swirling through the air in ever-increasing amounts and the hail had begun to pile in lumpy drifts along the curb. It had flattened the flowers she'd so lovingly placed in the planters and buried their stubbly remnants under inches of white, icy crystals.

In the distance, the dog had its tail between its legs and was disappearing into the maelstrom. Unless the frightened animal responded to commands to return, there was no chance of anyone catching up to it.

Gregory took a deep breath and hollered, "Char-lie," but

Maya could tell he was wasting his breath. The soggy mongrel didn't even slow.

"Take the boy and head for the basement," Gregory yelled at her. Ducking inside, he had to put his shoulder to the heavy door and use his full weight to close and latch it.

She shoved Tommy back at him. "No. I have to go get Layla."

"In this weather? Don't be an idiot."

"She's my daughter. She's only three. She'll be scared to death if I'm not there."

"She's in the preschool at the church, right? They'll take care of the kids."

"No. I'm going after her."

"Use your head. You can't help Layla if you get yourself killed." He grasped her wrist, holding tight.

Maya struggled, twisting her arm till it hurt. "Let me go. I'm going to my baby. She's all I've got."

"That's crazy! A tornado is coming. If the hail doesn't knock you out cold, the tornado's likely to bury you."

"I don't care."

"Yes, you do."

"No, I don't! Let go of me." To her amazement, he held fast. No one, especially a man, was going to treat her this way and get away with it. No one.

"Stop. Think," he shouted, staring at her as if she were deranged.

She continued to struggle, to refuse to give in to his will, his greater strength. "No. *You* think. I'm going to my little girl. That's all there is to it."

"How? Driving?" He indicated the street, which now looked distorted due to the vibrations of the front window. "It's too late. Look at those cars. Your head isn't half as hard as that metal is and it's already full of dents."

"But…"

She knew in her mind that he was right, yet her heart kept

insisting she must do something. Anything. *Please, God, help me. Tell me what to do!*

Her heart was still pounding, her breath shallow and rapid, yet part of her seemed to suddenly accept that her boss was right. That couldn't be. She belonged with Layla. She was her mother.

"We're going to take shelter," Gregory ordered, giving her arm a tug. "Now."

That strong command was enough to renew Maya's resolve and wipe away the calm assurances she had so briefly embraced. She didn't go easily or quietly. Screeching, "No, no, no," she dragged her feet, stumbling along as he pulled and half dragged her toward the basement access.

Staring into the storm moments ago, she had felt as if the fury of the weather was sucking her into a bottomless black hole. Her emotions were still trapped in those murky, imaginary depths, still floundering, sinking, spinning out of control. She pictured Layla, with her silky, long dark hair and beautiful brown eyes.

"If anything happens to my daughter I'll never forgive you!" she screamed at him.

"I'll take my chances."

Maya knew without a doubt that she'd meant exactly what she'd said. If her precious little girl was hurt she'd never forgive herself for not trying to reach her. To protect her. And she'd never forgive Gregory Garrison for preventing her from making the attempt. *Never.*

She had to blink to adjust to the dimness of the basement as he shoved her in front of him and forced her down the wooden stairs.

She gasped, coughed. The place smelled musty and sour, totally in character with the advanced age of the building. How long could that bank of brick and stone stores and offices stand against a storm like this? If these walls ever started to topple, nothing would stop their total collapse. Then it wouldn't matter whether they were outside or down here. They'd be just as dead.

That realization sapped her strength and left her almost without sensation. When her boss let go of her wrist and slipped his arm around her shoulders to guide her into a corner next to an abandoned elevator shaft, she was too emotionally numb to continue to fight him. All she could do was pray and continue to repeat, "Layla, Layla," over and over again.

"We'll wait it out here," he said. "This has to be the strongest part of the building."

Maya didn't believe a word he said.

Tommy's quiet sobbing, coupled with her soul-deep concern for her little girl, brought tears to her eyes. She blinked them back, hoping she could control her emotions enough to fool the boy into believing they were all going to come through the tornado unhurt.

As for her, she wasn't sure. Not even the tiniest bit.

All she could think about was her daughter. *Dear Lord, are You watching out for Layla? Please, please, please! Take care of my precious little girl.*

* * * * *

See the rest of Maya and Greg's story when
HEALING THE BOSS'S HEART *hits the shelves in July 2009.*
And be sure to look for all six of the books in the
AFTER THE STORM *series, where you can follow the residents of High Plains, Kansas, as they rebuild their town—and find love in the process.*

Love Inspired®

HEARTWARMING INSPIRATIONAL ROMANCE

Experience stories
centered on love and faith
with a variety of romances
just for you,
with 10 books every month!

Love Inspired®:
Enjoy four contemporary,
heartwarming romances every month.

Love Inspired® *Historical:*
Travel to a different time with two powerful
and engaging stories of romance, adventure
and faith every month.

Love Inspired® *Suspense:*
Enjoy four contemporary tales of intrigue
and romance every month.

Steeple
Hill®

*Available every month wherever books are
sold, including most bookstores, supermarkets,
drugstores and discount stores.*

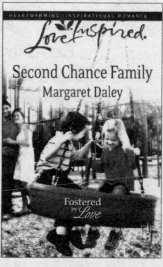

REQUEST YOUR FREE BOOKS!

2 FREE INSPIRATIONAL NOVELS
PLUS 2
FREE
MYSTERY GIFTS

Love Inspired®

YES! Please send me 2 FREE Love Inspired® novels and my 2 FREE mystery gifts (gifts are worth about $10). After receiving them, if I don't wish to receive any more books, I can return the shipping statement marked "cancel". If I don't cancel, I will receive 4 brand-new novels every month and be billed just $4.24 per book in the U.S. or $4.74 per book in Canada. That's a savings of over 20% off the cover price. It's quite a bargain! Shipping and handling is just 50¢ per book.* I understand that accepting the 2 free books and gifts places me under no obligation to buy anything. I can always return a shipment and cancel at any time. Even if I never buy another book, the two free books and gifts are mine to keep forever.

113 IDN EYK2   313 IDN EYLE

Name	(PLEASE PRINT)
Address	Apt. #
City	State/Prov.	Zip/Postal Code

Signature (if under 18, a parent or guardian must sign)

Mail to Steeple Hill Reader Service:
IN U.S.A.: P.O. Box 1867, Buffalo, NY 14240-1867
IN CANADA: P.O. Box 609, Fort Erie, Ontario L2A 5X3

Not valid to current subscribers of Love Inspired books.

Want to try two free books from another series?
Call 1-800-873-8635 or visit www.morefreebooks.com

* Terms and prices subject to change without notice. Prices do not include applicable taxes. Sales tax applicable in N.Y. Canadian residents will be charged applicable provincial taxes and GST. Offer not valid in Quebec. This offer is limited to one order per household. All orders subject to approval. Credit or debit balances in a customer's account(s) may be offset by any other outstanding balance owed by or to the customer. Please allow 4 to 6 weeks for delivery. Offer available while quantities last.

Your Privacy: Steeple Hill Books is committed to protecting your privacy. Our Privacy Policy is available online at www.SteepleHill.com or upon request from the Reader Service. From time to time we make our lists of customers available to reputable third parties who may have a product or service of interest to you. If you would prefer we not share your name and address, please check here. ☐

LIREG09

TITLES AVAILABLE NEXT MONTH
Available June 30, 2009

SECOND CHANCE FAMILY by Margaret Daley
Fostered by Love

Whitney Maxwell is about to get a lesson in trust—and family—from an unexpected source: her student Jason. As she and his single dad, Dr. Shane McCoy, try to help Jason deal with his autism, she realizes her dream of a forever family is right in front of her.

HEALING THE BOSS'S HEART by Valerie Hansen
After the Storm

When a tornado strikes her small Kansas town, single mom Maya Logan sees an unexpected side of her boss. Greg Garrison's tender care for her family and an orphaned boy make her wonder if he's hiding a family man beneath his gruff exterior.

LONE STAR CINDERELLA by Debra Clopton

The town matchmakers have cowboy Seth Turner in mind for history teacher Melody Chandler, but all he seems to want to do is stop her from researching his family history. Seth's afraid of what she'll find, especially when he realizes it's a place in his heart.

BLUEGRASS BLESSINGS by Allie Pleiter
Kentucky Corners

Cameron Rollings may be a jaded city boy, but God led him to Kentucky for a reason, and baker Dinah Hopkins plans to help him count his bluegrass blessings.

HOMETOWN COURTSHIP by Diann Hunt

Brad Sharp fully expects his latest community service volunteer, Callie Easton, to slack off on their Make-a-Home project. But her golden heart and willingness to work makes Brad take a second look, one that could last forever.

RETURN TO LOVE by Betsy St. Amant

Penguin keeper Gracie Broussard needs to find a new home for her beloved birds. If only Carter Alexander, the man who broke her heart years ago, wasn't the only one who could help. Carter promises that he's changed, and he's determined to show Gracie that love is a place you can always return to.

LICNMBPA0609